She'd been warned, Grace realized

But she'd fallen for the first real cowboy she'd met. Jack was helping her out of her car and kissing her at the same time, which might have been because she still had her arms around his neck. He backed her against the car, his wonderful mouth on hers, his hands on her shoulders, his body warm and solid.

"Crazy," he muttered, lifting his mouth.

"Us or the place?" She was afraid he was going to step away, and her heart sank as he did exactly that.

"Both." He took her hand and led her toward the house. "I don't want to make love to you against a car."

"No?"

"No." Grace thought she heard tenderness in his voice. "I like beds or haymows, take your pick."

"I've never made love in a haymow before."

He stopped in the middle of the driveway and looked down at her with a fierce expression in his dark eyes. "Tomorrow," he promised. "Tonight we use a bed."

Kristine Rolofson is one busy and amazing lady. The author of over twenty books, all published by Harlequin, she is also the mother of six! A Rhode Island native, she now resides in the same town where she spent her childhood. Writing about family life is one of the strong themes in her books. *Romantic Times* gave *The Texan Takes a Wife* a 4$\frac{1}{2}$ Gold Star (their very highest rating) and had this to say: "Jampacked with vividly appealing characters, this romantic romp captivates our hearts and delivers extraordinary reading bliss."

Kristine's story *A Touch of Texas* will be part of the Hometown Reunion series in March. She will also have a Love & Laughter book available in the fall of 1997.

Books by Kristine Rolofson

HARLEQUIN TEMPTATION
507—PLAIN JANE'S MAN
548—JESSIE'S LAWMAN
560—MAKE-BELIEVE HONEYMOON
569—THE COWBOY
604—THE TEXAN TAKES A WIFE
617—THE LAST MAN IN MONTANA (Boots & Booties)
621—THE ONLY MAN IN WYOMING (Boots & Booties)

Don't miss any of our special offers. Write to us at the following address for information on our newest releases.

Harlequin Reader Service
U.S.: 3010 Walden Ave., P.O. Box 1325, Buffalo, NY 14269
Canadian: P.O. Box 609, Fort Erie, Ont. L2A 5X3

Kristine Rolofson
THE NEXT MAN IN TEXAS

Harlequin Books

TORONTO • NEW YORK • LONDON
AMSTERDAM • PARIS • SYDNEY • HAMBURG
STOCKHOLM • ATHENS • TOKYO • MILAN
MADRID • WARSAW • BUDAPEST • AUCKLAND

With love to the newest baby in the family,
McKenna Kathryn Jacobson. Your Great-Auntie Kristine
can't wait to meet you.

ISBN 0-373-25725-2

THE NEXT MAN IN TEXAS

Copyright © 1997 by Kristine Rolofson.

DON'T FALL IN LOVE *with a cowboy.*

The words echoed in Grace Daniels's head as she drove toward Locklin, Texas, with a sleeping baby and a carload of baby apparatus. Her neighbor Lucy had loved to give advice. She would shake her head sorrowfully, blow a perfect smoke ring and roll her blue-shadowed eyes toward the ceiling.

They'll always break your heart, honey. Just like the song says.

Well, Grace figured, that much was true. At least in Lucy's case. Lucy, a thirty-something redhead with azure eyes, had had more experience with cowboys and broken hearts than Grace could imagine in her wildest dreams. In fact, Grace didn't have wild dreams, had never loved a cowboy, and her heart was nicely insulated from aching of any kind. And she intended to stay that way, too, though at times she had envied Lucy's breezy life-style and live-for-the-moment attitude.

But living for the moment didn't fit with raising a child. Lucy had done the best she could under the circumstances. She'd lived long enough to make Grace promise to deliver little Mac to his cowboy daddy. Lucy could convince anyone to do practically anything, even a shy computer programmer who preferred plants to people.

Grace turned up the air-conditioning, made sure the vents weren't directed toward the baby and headed south on Interstate 35. The sooner she got there, the sooner she could go home. All she had to do was find someone called McLintock, give him his son, break the news about Lucy and tiptoe quietly back to her car. She wasn't good at emotional moments, but she'd do her best.

He was a real charmer, that man was. Just about broke my heart when he left, but I got over it soon enough. Hearts mend, Gracie. They always do, sooner or later.

Grace squinted against the afternoon sun. She was tired of driving. She hadn't had much sleep last night; she'd been worried about driving close to three hundred miles with a six-month-old baby, but little Mac had been as well behaved as always. He went to sleep with a smile on his chubby face and woke up that way, too. Grace yawned. She would find a nice hotel room in San Antonio and tour the Alamo in the morning before heading back to Dallas. She didn't know why she'd never taken the time to see it before.

Mac gurgled, so Grace looked over to him and smiled. "Hey there, sweetheart. You ready to meet your daddy?"

The baby smiled as if he knew what she was talking about.

"He's going to be real happy to see you," she promised. And hoped she was right.

He told me he liked the idea of having sons. Guess he

should get the chance to raise this one, don't you think, Gracie?

Yes, Grace definitely thought Mr. McLintock should raise his own son. Lucy had come to the right person to agree with that particular statement. While it wasn't like her to leave home without a Triple A map and one of those thick books of hotel listings, Grace knew she had been given a mission to carry out. Mr. McLintock was about to get his baby back.

"PUT THE LITTLE son of a gun in the barn." Jack McLintock had run out of patience. "I've had just about enough for one day."

"Yes, boss." Jethro grinned and led the prancing two-year-old gelding out of the corral. "Anything you say, boss."

"Shut up, Jet."

"Yes, sir." He saluted as he walked past, and his battered hat tilted to reveal a pale forehead and a shock of dark hair.

Jack shook his head. "They're not going to know what to do with you in Nashville, you know."

"They'll learn," his brother assured him. "Don't you think?"

"Yeah," Jack said. "They'll learn, all right." He stepped back as the horse passed by him. Yesterday he'd learned that the gelding had a mean kick, and he didn't need to be reminded again.

Jethro called over his shoulder. "I'm cleaning up and going to town. You want to come? There's always a steak special at Nellie's on Friday night, then we're playing at the Stampede from nine to two."

"No, thanks. I've got—"

"Work to do," Jethro finished for him. "You work too hard."

"We all do."

"We all *did*."

"It's not over yet." Jack shrugged away the feeling that nothing was going to be the same again. They'd waited a long time for this summer to arrive. In a few weeks—exactly two weeks from today—everything would change. For the better. The relief almost made him dizzy. The anticipation was sometimes too much to bear.

"'It's All Over But the Shouting,'" Jethro said.

"Is that the name of your latest song?"

"Yep. I wrote it last night. Gonna try it out on the crowd during the second set, before everyone's too drunk to know what they're listening to."

"Sounds like a plan."

"Hell, yes," Jet agreed. "You should come down, have a beer, hear the band. We've got some new songs."

Jack shrugged. "Yeah, maybe," he said, but he knew he wouldn't.

"Well, think about it," Jet said, moving away. He whistled as he led the horse down the road to the largest barn on the place.

Jack turned away and headed toward the house. He could taste the dust, but that was nothing new. Just part of the job. He'd been running this ranch for so long that he'd gotten so he almost liked the taste. Jack tried to whistle, but his mouth was too dry to come up with anything but a pathetic rasping sound. He didn't know how Jethro did it, but that boy could make music in the middle of a dust storm.

Isabella sat fanning herself on the back porch. "Lord, it's hot," she said. "Too hot for June."

"It's always hot in June." He pushed his hat off his forehead and leaned against one of the posts. "I smell something good."

The old woman fanned herself with her apron and shrugged. "I would cook you something that smelled bad?"

Jack smiled at the familiar question. "No, Bella, in twenty years you have never cooked anything that smelled bad. 'Cept for that time you burned the—"

"Oh, hush your teasing."

"What are you going to do when you retire, Bella?"

The old woman gave him a dark look. "I don't like that word. And I'm not going to discuss it with a dirty, sweaty cowboy."

He bent over and brushed some of the dust from his jeans. "Better?"

She nodded. "You've got company. In the living room."

"Who?"

Isabella smiled. Jack figured she was seventy, easy. Maybe closer to eighty. "I don't know. I'm just an old cook who burns things."

Jack sighed and walked past her. "You and Jet are in good moods today. The two of you could get more work done if you weren't looking for ways to tease people all the time."

She muttered something, but didn't leave her seat on the porch. Jack went into the kitchen and peered into the pot on the stove. Ah. His favorite. Next to the oven, a stack of freshly made tortillas sat under a cotton cloth. He turned away from the food and walked down the hall to the large room that ran the length of the house. He stopped when he reached the doorway and saw a slim young woman standing in front of the fireplace. She was looking at the framed photographs that lined the wooden mantel, but when his boots clicked on the tiled floor, she turned around.

"Hello," he said, removing his hat. "What can I do for you, miss?" Gray eyes studied him. She didn't smile at first, but then a rose-tinted pair of lips turned upward and she moved forward, holding out her hand. He didn't recognize her, and wondered if he should. She could be one of Old Bill's lawyers, but he knew he hadn't seen her before. He would have remembered.

"Hi. I'm Grace Daniels."

Not a lawyer, or she would have said so. He took her hand as gently as he could and released it quickly. He didn't want to get her dirty. "Jack McLintock."

She nodded. "Yes, that's what I thought."

"You did?"

"Absolutely. I'm sorry to come here with no warning, but I tried to call from Locklin. The line was busy."

"Isabella takes it off the hook when she's fixing dinner."

Her expression clouded. "Oh. Your wife. I hadn't thought of that."

"Hadn't thought of what?" He ignored the mention of a wife and gestured at the brown leather couch. "Would you like to sit down?" He hoped she would. The woman, this Grace Daniels, had a fragile look about her. Maybe it was the flowered sundress, or the way her chestnut hair brushed her bare shoulders, or the white sandals that encased her tiny feet. She was pale and slender, the kind of woman who didn't spend much time outdoors and made a man feel hot and sweaty just to look at her.

"I'm sorry," she said again. "I'm just realizing how complicated this could be, and I can't believe I didn't think of it sooner."

"Complicated?" He could think of other words to describe having a beautiful stranger sitting in his living room on a Friday evening.

She waved her hand toward the overstuffed chair that sat by the window. "This is Mac. I brought him as soon as I could."

Jack's gaze dropped to the floor, where a chubby baby sat nestled in one of those thick plastic car seats. His eyes were closed, and his head was tilted at an angle that looked anything but comfortable.

"Mac looks tired" was the only thing he could think to say. Maybe Grace was one of Jet's friends, though she didn't look like the type to hang out in cowboy bars.

"We've come from Dallas today," she explained. "I

thought it was best that I bring him to you right away. Before I got too attached to him."

"Excuse me," he said, moving toward the couch again. He waited for her to sit down before he sat in the rocking chair across from her. "You're saying you brought this baby here? Why?"

"Lucy Bagwell passed away three days ago. Of cancer." She cleared her throat and hesitated, almost as if she expected him to say something. "Before she died she asked me to make sure that Mac got to his father. She didn't want him to end up in foster care."

He waited for her to continue, but she just looked at him. "And?" he prompted.

"Lucy Bagwell. You don't remember her?"

"I'm sorry, but I don't think I know anyone named Bagwell. Maybe you have the wrong place. Or the wrong man."

"No, I don't think so. I looked in the phone book and yours was the only McLintock listed." She flushed. "I'm really afraid I've done this the wrong way, but hiring a lawyer seemed so cold and impersonal, and I wanted to see for myself that Mac would be all right with his father."

Jack leaned forward. He dreaded the answer to his next question, but it had to be asked. And answered. "And exactly who on this ranch is supposed to be his father?"

"You, of course."

He couldn't say anything for long seconds. Then he drew in a deep breath and prayed for patience. "Lady, you're barking up the wrong tree."

"You're saying you didn't *know* about him?"

"If I were a father, I'd think I'd know it."

Grace gulped and reached for a large tote bag. She reached in and pulled out a piece of paper, then leaned forward to hand it to him. "All this time I thought you knew. Here, I think this explains it," she said, her voice soft. "It's Mac's birth certificate."

Jack took the paper and examined it. *Mother: Lucy Ann Bagwell, birth date April 23, 1961. Place of birth: Dallas, Texas. Father: J. McLintock. Place of birth: Locklin, Texas.* No birth date for the father, which sure as hell complicated things. He didn't know if this was a fraud or not. He didn't know which brother to tar and feather. "Are you sure about this?"

"As sure as I can be. It's the only record I have. Lucy didn't leave much else."

He held it up to the light. Sure enough, the damn thing had a seal pressed in the corner. Though, that didn't make the information on it 100 per cent accurate, either. "Mind if I make a copy?"

"No, of course not."

Jack stood up. He was going to make several copies and present them to each of his brothers before daybreak tomorrow. "I'll be right back. I have a copy machine in the office."

Grace stood, too. "Do you mind if I come with you? That's an original."

"Of course not." He didn't blame her for being careful, but he had no intention of destroying the damn thing and making a bad situation worse. She bent over and picked up the sleeping baby, plastic seat and all, and followed him down the hall to the office.

"It'll take a minute to warm up," he said, switching the button on. He took the baby, seat and all, from her and sat him on top of the papers on his desk. "How old is he?"

"Almost six months."

Add nine months to that, turn the clock back fifteen months, and see where the boys were. Should be simple to find out what was going on a year ago last March. That is, if one of them was involved. It was hard to imagine any of the boys being so careless. Damn it, he'd lectured them often enough. Jack examined the birth certificate again, this time looking for where and when the boy was born.

Mac started to cry, and the woman had him out of the seat and into her arms within seconds—she obviously cared for the boy. Jack turned away from them and made his copies. He handed her the original. "I'll look into this," he said, motioning for her to precede him into the hall. "Why is he crying like that?"

"He must be hungry."

"Do you, ah, have something to give him?"

"I have bottles in the cooler in my car. I also brought his fold-up bed and high chair, plus two boxes of clothes. Would you take him, please, so I can get him something to eat?"

He didn't want to take the child, but before Jack could protest, Mac was thrust into his arms. Twenty pounds of sobbing baby didn't faze Jack. He'd changed more diapers than he could count. He adjusted his grip on the boy. "Hey, kid, go easy on my eardrums."

Mac hiccuped and stared up at the stranger. Two tears ran down his red cheeks, but he stopped screaming.

"Thanks," Jack told him. "It's the end of a long week, and I could use a break, all right? You're going to have your dinner, and pretty soon I'm going to have my dinner." *Then in the morning I'll find your father and figure out what to do about you.* Jack walked over to the window and watched as the woman fumbled in the back seat of the Ford Taurus sedan. She didn't seem like the type to run off and leave the kid, but it wouldn't hurt to keep an eye on her, just in case.

She might be telling the truth. Or she might not. He wasn't going to take any chances. Locklin was a small town. People talked. And he was sure not going to give anyone anything more to say about the McLintock family.

GRACE HURRIED TO THE CAR and retrieved a bottle and a blanket. The inside of the ranch house had been air-conditioned. She didn't want Mac to catch cold. Meeting Mac's handsome father had been an experience, especially since the man seemed sincere when he'd said he didn't even know he had a son. What on earth had Lucy been thinking, if she hadn't told the father that he *was* a father? And the fact that he was married had been another surprise, but maybe Isabella would fall in love with Mac and want to keep him.

And maybe Santa would put diamonds in her stocking this year, too.

She arrived back in the living room to find Mac comfortable and quiet against the rancher's wide chest. Yes, Lucy hadn't exaggerated. From his dusty boots to those chiseled cheekbones, the McLintock man was clearly the kind of cowboy that would make a woman like Lucy salivate.

"He settled right down," the man said.

"Mac's probably happy to be out of that seat." Grace lifted her gaze to Mr. McLintock's chin. Sure enough, there was a cleft there. Mac had it already. In fact, they had the same dark brown hair, the same questioning expression in their dark eyes as they looked at her.

"What's wrong?" the man asked.

"Nothing." She attempted a smile. "I need to heat this bottle."

"Follow me."

He led her out of the room, past an enormous dining room filled with thick pine furniture and down a hall to a bright kitchen. Life wasn't fair sometimes, which wasn't exactly a revelation. She hadn't wanted to get involved in this situation. She knew she could have called the state authorities and let them handle this, but she couldn't risk Mac being put in foster care. Early this morning she had spent an anxious hour drinking a pot of coffee and wrestling with her conscience. Her conscience had won. She had promised Lucy to deliver Mac to his father and that is what she would do. Had done.

If Mr. McLintock refused to raise his own son, he

would have a fight on his hands. Mac deserved to have a father. His *own* father.

"Isabella," the rancher called. An old woman, her gray hair hanging in a braid, stood by the stove stirring something in a steaming pot. The woman turned and stared at the baby in his arms.

"Ah," she sighed, reaching one bony finger to touch the child's chin. "Another McLintock. Whose?"

"I don't know," McLintock muttered. "This is Grace Daniels. She has quite a story to tell." He didn't smile. "Grace, come meet Isabella Moniz. She runs things around here and also makes fifty-eight different kinds of chili."

"Fifty-nine," the woman said. She smiled at Grace but didn't move from the stove. "You are staying for supper, miss?"

"No, but thank you for the invitation." So Isabella wasn't the wife, after all. Grace knew she had to stop jumping to conclusions. "Can I put this bottle in some hot water, please?" Mac whimpered and squirmed when she held up the bottle, but Mr. McLintock didn't seem to be the least uncomfortable holding him.

"Sure," he said, moving out of the way so she could reach the sink.

"A pot," the woman said, placing one battered pot in the sink. Grace filled it with water and put the bottle inside to warm.

"Where are you going?"

"Back to Dallas."

"Tonight?"

"No. I'm going to San Antonio tonight. I always wanted to see the Al—"

"With or without this child?"

"Without." Her gaze dropped to Mac, who gave her that *where's my supper* look. She ignored the pang in her heart and turned back to the bottle. It would be warm enough by now. She sprinkled a few drops on her wrist just to make sure. "I've done what I promised to do."

He put the baby in her arms while Isabella watched with undisguised interest. "No, lady, I don't think you have."

"Meaning?" Grace didn't wait for an invitation to sit down. There were several pine chairs arranged around a long trestle table, so she sat in one and gave Mac his bottle. The rancher took a chair and placed it across from her, then sat down.

"Meaning, I'm not the boy's father."

"You want dinner now?" Isabella called.

"No. Not yet. Not till I get this straightened out."

"Hah," the cook snorted. "You'll have to wait a long time for *that*. That boy has the chin, he does. And there's no telling where he got it, either." She shook her head as she looked at Mac, then she went outside through the back door.

Grace was hot and tired and thirsty, and she had to go to the bathroom. She wished she had stayed in Dallas. She wished Lucy was still around to tell stories and give her advice that she would never need to use. Mac drank with noisy slurps, then she sat him on her lap and awkwardly burped him.

"What do you want?" the man asked.

"I want what's best for Mac. I promised to bring him to his father." She studied the man's expression. He was handsome, with those dark eyes and short brownish black hair. Jack McLintock looked the part of a Texas rancher, all right. He was covered in dust, dirt streaked one side of his face, and his jaw was square and set in an uncompromising position. *That boy has the chin,* the old woman had said.

He sure did.

"Are you his father?" It was a simple question. Grace assumed he'd tell the truth.

"No."

"Are there any other McLintocks I could talk to about this?"

"I'll take care of that," he said.

"I can't leave him until I know he's going to be all right. I have to contact Lucy's lawyer when I get back and—"

"Lady, you're not going anywhere. Not until this is straightened out."

"I really can't do that."

"You don't have any choice. I'm not the baby's father, so you haven't delivered him to the father. Right?"

"How do I know you're telling the truth?"

He smiled grimly. "You don't. But you and I know you can't leave this child with strangers. You drive out of here and I call Children's Services and have that boy put in their custody until we get to the bottom of this."

"You would do that?"

He leaned forward. "I'm sure as hell not going to

baby-sit someone else's kid while a woman I've never seen blackmails me into taking responsibility for him."

"He's not yours?"

"The McLintocks aren't known to be family men. You've walked into the wrong place."

Grace's arms tightened around the child. She had done her best. She could take Mac and go home now. And she would do her best to make sure that little Mac grew up safe and happy and healthy. "Okay," she agreed. "I'll have my lawyer call you if there are any problems with the adoption process."

His eyes narrowed. "Adoption process?"

"Yes." She put Mac up to her shoulder and stood. "If you don't want him, I'll find a nice childless couple who does."

"I didn't say I didn't want him. I said I wasn't his father." He stood, too, and looked down at her as he put his hands on his hips. "I'm not a liar, and I never heard of Lucy Bagwell, but I intend to find out who's going around writing 'McLintock' on birth certificates."

"If you're not his father, you can't—"

McLintock smiled, as if amused by her innocence. "Lady, there are other McLintocks here. You're staying and Mac is staying until we figure out what the hell is going on."

"*Other* McLintocks?" Oh, heavens. What on earth had she gotten herself into?

"Yeah."

Grace pretended that she was still in control of the situation. "Can I talk to them, please?"

"You'll meet them all soon enough, but for right

now, this little problem stays between us. I don't want everyone in town talking about the McLintock bastard."

Grace gulped. "I'm sure I don't want that, either, Mr. McLintock."

"Jack," he corrected her. "Call me Jack. I don't want you talking about this with the boys, either. That's my job. From now on you're a distant cousin of my mother's from Dallas who's here for the party. Mac here is your son. You've just gotten a divorce."

"I have?"

"Yeah. If anyone asks, just say that Jess McLintock was your mother's third cousin."

"Who's that?"

"My mother."

"She won't mind?"

"She's dead," he said, and the tiniest shadow of pain crossed his face.

"I'm sorry."

He shrugged. "It happened a long time ago. Now, people won't be coming here for the party yet, but as far as my brothers are concerned—"

"A party?" Grace wished she could retrace her steps, reconsider this morning's decision and fade quietly back into the woodwork.

"My youngest brother is turning twenty-one in a couple of weeks. We're having a big shindig to celebrate."

Brothers. She hadn't thought of that, either. Grace sighed. She had been spending too much time at her computer and not enough time in the real world. There could have been a wife, but thank goodness there wasn't. There could have been other McLintocks, and there were. Brothers. Jack McLintock could be lying about not fathering a child or he could be telling the truth, but she really had no choice but to go along with this. For Mac's sake, anyway. If he had a father here on the ranch, then he should have the chance to be seen by him.

Grace squared her shoulders. "How many brothers?"

"Three."

She had a sinking feeling in her chest. "And their names?"

He leveled that steady gaze on her. "Jethro, Jimmy-Joe and Jason," the McLintock man drawled. "Not going to be as easy as you thought, is it."

"What about cousins, uncles, brothers-in-law?"

Jack McLintock shook his head. "Nope. It's the four of us. We're the last of the line."

"Not exactly."

His eyebrows rose. "Maybe. All you have is a baby and a birth certificate."

"And that baby has the McLintock chin. Anyone can see the resemblance."

"We'll see," he said. "Let me show you to a room."

"I could stay in town," she offered, not comfortable with the idea of staying in a stranger's house.

"No way. The less you and Mac are seen in town, the better. I don't want any of this to get out and spoil Jason's party. He just graduated from college. With honors. And a chance to study in England."

"Really? That's impressive."

"He's the smartest McLintock I've ever seen. Takes after my mother. She liked to read, too. When she had the time."

Before Grace could ask him anything else, he led her down a hall into a separate wing of the house and into a bright corner room on the first floor. The floor was tiled and dotted with faded rag rugs. There was a single bed covered with a bright blue cotton spread, a pine chest of drawers and a ladder-backed chair.

"I'll bring in the baby's things from your car," Mc-Lintock said. "Do you think you'll need anything else?"

She needed a glass of wine and a few days' vacation, but she'd settle for a washcloth and a chance to change Mac's diaper. "Can you tell me where the bathroom is?"

"Down the hall, the second door on your right. Ask Isabella to get you anything you need." He glanced at Mac, who rested his head on Grace's shoulder and stared at the cowboy with big brown eyes.

"Just Mac's bed for now, thank you."

He nodded. "I'll be right back." And he left her there, holding the baby and gazing out the window into an enormous courtyard. *Courtyard?* Grace stepped closer to the window, which she noticed was actually a narrow door that led outside. A wheelbarrow stood in the middle, as if someone had been weeding or digging. Pots of flowers sat to one side as if they were waiting to be planted. The house was a Spanish design; the walls were adobe and appeared old. It was the kind of home she'd dreamed of as a child, the kind in magazines where beautiful mothers and handsome fathers smiled at each other and their sweet-looking children. It was the kind of place she'd longed to belong to, but that had never happened, and never would.

"How about that?" she asked the baby. "You might be living in a real hacienda." Mac's head lay heavy on her shoulder, and he seemed content to be held. His little legs were relaxed, and one hand played with her hair. "Your name will be Mac McLintock. You'll have a daddy and maybe your own horse. Won't that be nice?"

Grace wished Mac could talk and agree with her so she would feel better about leaving him. There was nothing to stop her from leaving and taking the child with her. Nothing but a birth certificate, a promise to Lucy and a very large cowboy. He could call the sheriff, could accuse her of kidnapping. He might not want a scandal, but he wanted the truth.

She would stay for tomorrow, until she found Mac's father. She wasn't leaving until she'd done what she'd promised Lucy. Little Mac was going to have a family.

2

"WHERE'S JET?"

One of the men looked up from his supper. "Gone to town, I guess. He's playin' at the Stampede tonight. You goin'?"

"No." Jack hid his disappointment. "I just thought I'd catch him before he left."

"Aw, he was outta here like a streak of greased lightnin'. He always moves fast on Fridays."

"Yeah, well, I'll catch up with him tomorrow, then." Jack backed out of the bunkhouse and left the men to their supper. They'd be heading to town as soon as they cleaned up. Friday night in Locklin was almost as good as Saturday night in Locklin.

No way was he spending all weekend trying to figure out this mess. No way was he getting stuck with a baby at this time of his life. Hell, he'd raised enough boys. He would have to talk to all three of them, though, just to make sure. Jimmy-Joe had taken off early, and Jason was late getting his college-educated ass home.

And he was left dealing with the Dallas woman and the McLintock baby. *"Hell,"* Jack swore out loud. He was already thinking of little Mac as a McLintock. Surely there were other babies with brown eyes and an unmistakable cleft in their chins. He walked back to the house and tried to convince himself that there were worse things in the world that could happen now. If that little boy was Jet's, then he could damn well support the child. He would be able to do that, at least financially, in two weeks.

He wondered if Grace Daniels knew about the McLintock trust fund. Or if Lucy Bagwell knew she was sending her baby to a family who would now be able to afford to feed one more.

Well, he wasn't going to sit around all night worrying about it. He knew exactly where Jet was going to be at nine o'clock tonight. As much as he hated hanging out at the Stampede, he was going to get this mess straightened out as soon as possible. Before people started to talk.

"SUPPER," ISABELLA SAID. She stood in the doorway to Grace's room. "Come. It's ready."

Grace hesitated. Mac was sleeping peacefully, his thumb tucked in his mouth and his freshly diapered bottom up in the air.

"He will be fine," the old woman assured her. "I will come back and listen for him while you eat."

"Are you sure you don't mind?"

"I like babies," the woman said. "I have seventeen grandchildren."

"That's wonderful." Grace followed her down the hall. "Do any of them live around here?"

"Some. My two oldest girls live in town. Another is

married to one of the hands here on the Double L. The other three are grown and have moved away."

"You have six children?" Grace wondered how the woman had managed. Just taking care of Mac these past weeks had turned her life upside down. "That's wonderful."

"You'll meet them. They are all coming next week, for the party."

Grace didn't point out that she would be leaving tomorrow. "That's nice," she said as Isabella led her back through the living room, dining room and kitchen.

"You can save yourself some steps and walk across the courtyard next time, if you want. Be careful where you walk, though. We are cleaning it up for the party."

"Sounds like it's going to be quite a celebration."

Isabella nodded, her face solemn, as she pointed out a place at the table that was set with bright pottery. "We have all waited a long time for this."

Jack McLintock shot Isabella a stern look. "Jason has worked hard to graduate from school," he said.

"Yes," the old woman said. "He is such a smart boy, always writing things on paper, always reading."

And making babies, too? Grace sat down at the table and put her napkin in her lap. "Where are the rest of your brothers, Mr. McLintock?"

"Call me Jack." He frowned, knowing exactly what she was asking. "Jet has gone to town. His band is playing in Locklin tonight."

"Could we go see him? The sooner we clear all this up, the better."

Isabella placed a large bowl of chicken stew in front of her. "Clear up what?"

"Thank you," Grace said. "It smells wonderful."

Jack shook his head. "Never mind, Bella."

The old woman laughed. "Oh, you're wondering where that baby got his McLintock chin, aren't you?"

Grace looked at Jack and waited for him to answer, but he ignored the question and Isabella returned to the table with a bowl for him.

"Green chicken chili," she said. "Not too hot."

"'Not too hot' could mean anything," the rancher warned. "So go easy on the first bite."

"Okay." She scooped up a small spoonful and tasted a piece of chicken and green sauce. It was spicy enough to make her throat burn, but the sensation wasn't unpleasant.

Isabella returned with a plate of tortillas and two bottles of beer. "There," she said, setting the bottles between them. "I'm going to sit with the little one while you eat." She turned to Jack. "I'll stay here tonight if you want to take the lady to meet Jethro."

"Thank you," Grace said, pleased that it was going to be easy to talk to another McLintock. "Are you sure you wouldn't mind?"

The housekeeper chuckled. "No, I love babies. I'll sit with him in his room while he sleeps. You'll like Jethro. He's a fine boy."

"No one's going anywhere," Jack said.

Grace ignored him and looked at Isabella. "Jethro is the singer?"

"Here." Jack twisted the top off of the beer bottle

and handed it to her. "If you're going to eat Bella's chili, you're going to need something cold."

Grace wasn't a beer drinker, but she took it, anyway. She didn't usually eat chili with cowboys or take care of babies, either, so what difference did a bottle of beer make? She took a couple of sips and then got back to the subject of the conversation. "I'd really like to meet your brother."

He waited for the cook to leave the kitchen before he answered. "I don't want you asking anyone any questions."

"I know that. But you're not exactly calling the shots."

"You're in my home, accusing me of fatherhood. I'd say that gives me the right to get to the bottom of this mess."

"I'm not leaving until I deliver this child to his father. I promised his mother, and that's what I'm going to do."

"And if you can't find out who the father is?"

"There are lawyers and blood tests and DNA."

"You're prepared to go that far?"

He didn't have any idea how far she was prepared to go. If he'd spent a couple of months in a bad foster home, he'd understand. Or even worse, if he'd ever been taken away from a loving foster mother and placed somewhere else, he'd know.

"If he's a McLintock, he should be raised as a McLintock," she declared.

Jack laughed. "That's a curse, not a blessing, sweetheart. We're not exactly the most stable family in

Texas. Ask anyone in Locklin. My father was in jail—
twice—and took off after Jason was born. My mother
died of overwork and a broken heart. Sure you want
Mac to join this family?"

"He deserves to have a name. Let me talk to Jethro
tonight."

"No."

"Why not?"

"It should be done man-to-man. In private."

"So the two of you can cook up some story? No
way."

Jack opened his mouth, but no sound came out. He
inhaled and exhaled slowly before answering. "You're
questioning my integrity?"

"I'm just saying that if you two are going to talk, I
should be there to listen. I won't say anything unless I
have to, but I should be there."

"How do you know I haven't already talked to
him?"

"You wouldn't be arguing with me if you had."

"If the boy is a McLintock, I'll see that his father
takes responsibility for him."

"Will he give him a home?"

"He doesn't have a home to give him. You want that
child raised on a tour bus?"

"Will he sign away his rights, then, so Mac can be
adopted?"

"By you?"

"No."

The man's eyebrows rose but he didn't say anything.
"Are you married?"

"No."

"Children?"

"No."

"And yet you're concerned about the little boy. Why?"

"His mother was my friend. It was important to her, my taking Mac to his father."

"But you haven't found him yet."

"I will."

"And then what?"

"Then I leave here and go back to Dallas."

"Promise?"

She nodded. "Promise."

"All right. We'll head to town at eight and see if we can talk to Jet before the first set."

"Good," she said, picking up her spoon. "I've never met a country-western singer before. Has he been doing it for a long time?"

"Yeah. He's going to Nashville in a couple of weeks."

"Is he famous?"

"Only around here."

"He's never played anywhere else in Texas?"

Jack McLintock drained his bottle of beer. "Save the questions for later, lady. Jet goes on stage at nine. We'll get to him before then."

Grace helped herself to a tortilla. She was on the right track now. It had taken her a little longer than she thought it would, but Lucy had loved honky-tonk bars and men who played guitars. Jethro McLintock had to be the one.

"HELL," JACK SWORE, pulling Grace into the crowded bar. The jukebox volume must have been turned to high. "You can't hear yourself think in this place."

"I should have worn jeans," she muttered, hanging back. "I'm not dressed for this."

"You're fine." He glanced down at her and hid a sigh. She was too damn pretty for this place. Jack surveyed the room and caught two or three men staring at Grace as if they'd never seen a woman before. He glared at one guy until the man turned back to his shot glass. Jack tightened his grip on Grace's hand. "Come on. I'll find a table for you, then I'll see if I can find Jet."

"You're going to leave me here alone?"

He released her hand and pulled a chair over to a small corner table for two. "You'll be fine. Just don't talk to anyone except the waitress."

She gave him a strange, questioning look, so he added, "Look, honey. You wanted to come here, so you're going to have to do things my way. Sit down, and by the time you order a drink I'll be back with Jet."

Grace sat down and surveyed the crowd. "Your brother must be very popular."

"It's like this on Friday nights whether Jethro is playing or not. Don't move. I'll get him and be right back."

"You won't talk to him about Mac?"

"Not unless you're hanging on every word."

She smiled, which made Jack even sorrier he'd brought her to a dump like the Stampede. She was the kind of woman a man took to a fancy restaurant with candles on the table and violin music. Of course, there weren't any places like that until you got to San Antonio. He tipped his hat to her and made his way through the crowd. He had to keep his mind on business, not on a pretty brunette with soft gray eyes.

Two of the guys were busy setting up the equipment when he approached the stage. "Hey, Tim, Gus."

Gus, the bass player, turned and grinned. "Hey, Jack. Jet didn't say that you were comin' tonight! You come to hear the new songs?"

"Not exactly. I've got to talk to Jet for a few minutes. Where is he?"

"He was out back unloading, but he came inside a few minutes ago and went off to talk to a couple of people." Gus looked at his watch. "We're going to start getting tuned up as soon as I get all this stuff plugged in. When I see him I'll tell him you're here."

"Thanks. Maybe I'll get lucky and find him first."

Tim chuckled. "Look for a group of women and he'll be in the middle."

Jack turned back to survey the room. The place was starting to fill up even more, the overflow moving onto the dance floor, where a handful of couples danced the two-step to the jukebox. They were lined up three deep at the bar on the other side of the building, and more were spilling in through the door. He couldn't see Grace; a group of cowboys stood showing off for a hard-looking blonde and blocked his view of the corner table. Either folks in the county were desperate to party or Jet and his band were drawing a big crowd. Jet should have been easy to spot, but the light was dim and the air smoky.

Jack made his way back to the table to find Grace talking to the waitress.

"One beer and one whiskey on the rocks, please."

"I don't drink whiskey," Jack said.

"Usually, neither do I," Grace informed him. "But this seemed like a good place for me to do it, don't you think?"

"Bring the lady a Coke, too," he told the waitress, then he pulled out a chair and sat down.

"Is it always like this here?"

"I wouldn't know. I'm not much for hanging around in bars."

She actually looked disappointed. "Neither am I. I thought I was with an expert and could learn something."

"What exactly did you want to learn?"

She shrugged those pretty shoulders, and Jack's gaze drifted down to her breasts for a brief, appreciative second. "I don't know," she said, looking around the room. "Lucy used to talk about the noise and the fun and the people. She worked as a cocktail waitress in a lot of places like this."

Which was exactly the right place to meet a guy like Jet, Jack thought. "Was she a big drinker?"

"Not that I know of. What are you getting at?"

"I was just thinking that she could have misunderstood the name of who she went to bed with."

Grace glared at him. "Lucy wasn't like that."

The waitress returned and set the drinks in front of them. Jack started to pull out his wallet, but the girl stopped him. "That's already been taken care of," she said.

"By who?"

"Me," a tall young man declared, stepping up to the table. He tucked a bill in the woman's apron. "Thank you, darlin'. I'll take over from here."

"Don't forget my song," she said, clearly impressed that Jet McLintock was taking the time to flirt with her.

"I won't. 'I Still Believe In You,' right?"

"That's the one." She moved away reluctantly and was immediately stopped by a group of rowdy cowboy lookalikes.

Jet grinned. "Everyone wants me to sing like Vince Gill."

"Sit down," Jack said, not smiling at his younger brother. He wanted to ask some questions, and he wanted some answers. And then he wanted to be able to send Grace and Mac back to Dallas to find the child's *real* father.

"Can't," Jet said. "We're starting at nine. If we're late starting we don't get free drinks during the first break." He turned to Grace and held out his hand. "Hi, there. I'm Jet, the good-looking McLintock."

She laughed and shook his hand. "Grace Daniels," she said. "You two look so much alike."

"But I'm the best-looking one. And I didn't know Jack had a date tonight." He released her hand and grinned at his brother. "Thought you weren't going out."

"It's not—"

"Hey, guys and gals!" a voice called over the microphone. "You all ready for a good time? You know who's here! Jet and the Naked Ladies!"

The crowd cheered and Jet laughed. "Gotta go." He tipped his hat toward Grace and winked. "They can't start without me. I'm the lead guitarist and singer."

"I need to talk to you." Jack gave his brother an I-mean-business look, but Jet stood up.

"I'll catch you between sets," he promised, turning to Grace. "Any requests from the lady?"

She looked surprised. "Really?"

Jet winked. "Yep. If I know it, I'll play it for you."

"How about 'Crazy'?"

"Willie Nelson?"

"Yes. But if you don't know it, then that's all right. Anything would be—"

"No problem, darlin'. One of my favorites, in fact." He grinned at Jack one more time. "You ought to date this lady again."

Jack ignored the romantic advice. "We'll wait for you."

"Right," he agreed, walking away, but Jack thought his brother could have taken the command a little more seriously.

"So that was Jet," Grace murmured. "Definitely Lucy's type, though a little on the young side."

"He's twenty-six. And, according to the birth certificate, Mac's mother would have been the same age as I am, thirty-six."

"That's a big age difference."

"Some women prefer it," he said, watching the way

the women in the crowd watched Jethro hop onto the stage.

"I meant between the two of you."

"Yeah, well, my father was doing time in the state penitentiary for a few years. Kind of interrupted his family life."

Grace took a sip from her whiskey glass. "And you and your mother worked on the ranch?"

"Yep. When the old man came home, he stuck it out for a few years. The boys were born and he took off again." He took a swallow of beer and studied the woman beside him. "Still sure you want that baby of yours to be part of the family?"

"He's not mine," she pointed out, but she gave him a look that made him feel guilty for being so blunt. But damn it, the woman needed to know what that child was getting into.

"For all I know, he's yours," she added. "Or Jet's. Someone has to take responsibility for him."

"No lectures, lady," Jack drawled, leaning back in his chair as the music started. "I wrote the book on responsibility, and now I'm on the final chapter."

"I'D LIKE TO DEDICATE this next song to the little lady who's crazy enough to go out with my older brother," Jet announced, waving one arm toward their table. People stared. Grace tried not to laugh at the expression on Jack's face. He wasn't happy being the center of attention, that was certain.

"Honey," Jet continued, "I hope you know what you're getting into."

The crowd applauded as Jet broke into the first verse of "Crazy," and the dance floor quickly filled with couples who wrapped themselves around each other for the slow dance.

"I suppose you want to dance to this one," Jack said, standing up.

He didn't have to sound so reluctant. "With you?"

He held out his hand. "There are two guys waiting to see if you're going to dance with me. If you refuse, they'll think you're fair game, and they'll be over here as soon as I excuse myself to go, uh, outside for a few minutes. You want that?"

Grace stood. "I'd like to dance, thank you."

"Thought so," he said, guiding her away from the table.

She stopped short. "Where's your beer bottle?"

"On the table. Why?"

"Could you bring it?" She pointed to the men dancing, their beer bottles hanging from their fingers behind their ladies' backs. "I've always wondered how that works."

"I usually don't drink and dance at the same time," he muttered, but he took his bottle and her hand.

"Me either," she said, but she figured she was going to like it. He led her onto the dance floor and took her into his arms. His right arm, bottle in hand, dangled from her shoulder, and his left encircled her waist. Grace was impressed.

"I'm not much of a dancer," McLintock said.

"You seem to be doing all right." She liked the way he held her. He seemed a lot larger now that she was touching him. When someone bumped her and pushed her against Jack's chest, she felt the warmth beneath his shirt and that hard chest. "Sorry," she said, righting herself.

"My fault," he said. "I should have seen him coming."

Grace, feeling shy again, fumbled for something to say. Dancing this close to such a big cowboy was turning her from an intelligent computer expert into a tongue-tied teenager. She looked over and saw Jet smiling at her. "Your brother is watching us."

"My brother has some explaining to do."

Grace hoped that Jet would take the news of his fatherhood well. She didn't think he seemed like the kind of man who would ignore the existence of a child, but since she'd only spoken to him for five minutes, she probably didn't have much of a handle on him. "Does Jet like children?"

"He likes everyone. And everyone likes him. Women, kids, horses and dogs, you name it and Jet will charm them."

"You don't call him Jethro?"

"Sometimes."

Grace listened to Jet's deep voice as he sang the song. He sounded just as good—or even better—than the singers she listened to on the radio while she worked. Add the McLintock good looks, including that square McLintock chin with the appealing cleft. He wore black jeans and a black T-shirt, with a black Stetson perched on top of his dark hair. He was tall and lean, not as wide-chested as Jack, but maybe a little taller. And definitely more outgoing.

The song ended, and the band went right into a faster number, something that made enthusiastic couples crowd the dance floor. Jack led her back to their table and politely held her chair for her.

He looked at his watch and then at her almost-full whiskey glass. "Jet should be through with this first set pretty soon. Want another drink?"

"No, thanks."

They sat in silence, waiting for Jet to return. When the set ended with a loud guitar flourish and a crashing of the drums, they watched Jet hop off the stage, grab a beer from a passing waitress and head their way. He hooked his foot around a chair leg and pulled it toward him, straddled it backward and grinned at Grace.

"What'd you think? Saw you two dancing out there."

"You have a great band," Grace told him. "Jack said you're going to Nashville soon?"

"Yep. In a couple of weeks. We've got the name of a guy to contact, we're going to make a demo tape, and then we're going to start making music. Stick around for a while. We're going to do some of the new numbers in the second set." He looked at his watch. "I gotta get back pretty soon. The owner doesn't like long breaks."

"I'll bet you'll be famous some—"

"Jet, do you know a woman named Lucy Bagwell?" Jack had leaned forward, his gaze on Jet's face.

The younger man shook his head. "Nope. I don't think so. Is she an agent or something?"

"No. She had a baby a few months ago, and she put a McLintock down on the birth certificate as being the father."

Jet chuckled. "Not me, Jack. I don't go around taking chances like that."

His brother didn't smile. "Not even once?"

"No." He turned to Grace, but this time Jet wasn't laughing. "I thought your name was Grace."

"It is," she said, scooting her chair closer so she could hear over the sound of the music coming from the jukebox. Jet looked so sincere that she almost felt sorry for him. "Lucy was my neighbor. She left the baby with me before she died. I came to town to bring Mac to his father."

He took a drink from the beer bottle. "What does this have to do with me?"

She had to give Jet credit for looking calm. "Where were you a year ago last March?"

Jet shrugged. "I don't know. I'll have to look it up. Gus keeps a record of where we've played and for how much."

"Find out" was all Jack said, but Jet looked as if he'd been given a command from up above.

"First thing in the morning," he promised.

"Grace is staying at the ranch," Jack added. "With the baby."

Jet's eyebrows rose as he turned to his brother. "No sh—kidding. You think there's a chance this could be legit? Have you talked to Jimmy?"

"Not yet."

"Damn. He can't take a baby with him to L.A."

Jack didn't look sympathetic, Grace noticed. "If it's his, he'll have to figure out something."

"Could you and Isabella keep—"

"No."

"I gotta get back," Jet said, swinging his leg over the chair. "The crowd gets ugly in between sets, and there'll be a fight in the parking lot, sure enough, if the music doesn't start soon." He hesitated, then leaned closer. "I'm not anyone's father, Jack. I swear."

"We'll talk in the morning," his older brother said. "We'll get to the bottom of this."

"Ma'am." Jet tipped his hat. "I wish you luck, but I'm not your man."

Grace wondered. She'd give a lot to see a record of where that band had played. Anyone with a band called the Naked Ladies must like women. And Jet had the kind of easy charm that Lucy would fall for.

"I'll finish this beer and we'll leave," Jack said.

"I'm in no hurry. I'd like to hear some of your brother's songs," she said. When else would she get the chance to hear a real country-western singer perform? Grace watched as Jet stepped up on stage. A group of young women hovered nearby and watched him with adoring expressions.

"You may want to hang around here, but I don't like crowds."

"Do you think he's telling the truth?"

"He's never lied to me before. Least, not since he was grown."

Jet's band roared to life and Grace couldn't hear the rest of what Jack said to her, but she thought she heard him ask her if she really wanted a McLintock to raise that child.

"DAMN, MAN, YOU CUT IT close. Old Burley gave me the evil eye for five minutes," Gus complained.

"I was talking to Jack," Jet said, slipping the guitar strap over his head. He tried out a few chords. Jet waved to the sound man, and got the thumbs-up sign. "He's here with a woman, a *pretty* woman."

"You know her?"

"Never saw her before." He looked over toward the table, but the shadows hid Jack's face. *Never heard of her friend Lucy, either.*

Gus chuckled and practiced a riff on the bass. "There's a pretty woman in Texas that you don't know? I can't believe it."

"She's from out of town. Jack didn't say from where." He wondered if that was deliberate.

"Maybe he's getting married. Now that you all are going on your way and all, he's found himself a woman."

"Jack? He doesn't go anywhere to meet women." Hell, his older brother sure wasn't being accused of fathering a child. "I don't remember the last time he had a date."

"We starting with 'All My Exes' or one of the new songs?"

"One of the new ones. Let's do 'Can't Take It Anymore.'" Gus nodded and told the rest of the guys. Jet glanced toward his brother one more time as the band started the intro. He didn't know how this was going to turn out, but he was sure glad to see Jack getting out and having a good time. Jack must like the little lady or he wouldn't have danced with her.

Everybody knew Jack didn't dance.

Jet launched into the opening bars and sang, "I can't take it anymore, but I want all you have to give," into the microphone. He kept his voice low, the way he knew the women liked it, and scanned the crowd.

"I can't take it anymore, when there's nothing for which I have to live." He made sure he looked tortured. Women loved it when a man looked like he was suffering from love.

A scuffle broke out in the corner near Jack's table, but Jet couldn't see through the crowd to find out what was going on. Then he spotted his brother, and a man fell against a table. He heard glass break and saw the two bouncers shove their way through the crowd.

"I can't take it, no, I can't take it."

Jet forgot about looking tortured and grinned. Friday night in Locklin, and Jack was finally getting into the swing of things.

3

"I'M SORRY." And she really meant the words. She'd said them at least three times since they'd left the bar, but the tall rancher hadn't said anything in response but *Don't worry about it.*

"Don't worry about it." Jack opened the refrigerator and rummaged through the contents. "Damn."

"Let me get it for you," Grace said. "I'll fix an ice pack."

"Not ice." He took out a flat package. "Steak."

"You're hungry?"

He sighed, shut the refrigerator door and turned around. "It's for the swelling." He tossed his hat on the table and sat down, then leaned back. He rested his head against the kitchen wall and held the white paper package of meat to his eye.

Since Jack looked like he had everything under control, Grace left the kitchen and hurried to the bedroom to check Mac. Isabella sat knitting in the chair while the baby slept in his little bed. The old woman put her finger to her lips.

"I just fed him," she whispered. "He ate like a McLintock, all right."

Grace had to smile at the woman's description. "Thank you for taking such good care of him."

"He's a sweet one." Isabella gathered her yarn and stuffed it into a faded tapestry bag, then followed Grace into the hall. "You found Jethro?"

"Yes." Grace shut the bedroom door behind her with a quiet click, and the two women walked back down the hall toward the other wing. They walked into the kitchen, and Isabella clucked her disapproval. "But there was a little bit of a problem before we left."

"Oh." The woman sighed. "There usually is."

Grace decided that Isabella's observation was probably true, at least from what she'd experienced tonight. Jack still leaned against the wall, but he took the steak from his face and peered at them through the eye that wasn't swollen shut. "You call this a 'little problem'?"

Isabella shrugged. "We've all seen worse. But I thought you were too old for bar fights. Thought you were old enough to know better."

"Yeah. Seems like there are a few things we all thought we knew better than what we did," he muttered.

Grace supposed that remark referred to Mac's arrival on earth.

Isabella sniffed. "Won't hurt you much to get out and have some fun, I suppose. If you can hold your temper."

"Last time I take Grace to a bar, I'll tell you that."

"The black eye isn't my fault," Grace protested, wishing she could back out of the kitchen and go to bed. She should have stayed with Mac, but she'd thought she should say good-night to her host.

Jack put the meat back on his face. "You smiled at the guy."

"I was being polite." The big man had said hello to her, and she had thought he was a friend of the McLintocks. She hadn't wanted to be rude, despite the leer on his big square face and the way his gaze had dropped to her chest.

"He thought you were encouraging him."

"You didn't have to hit him."

"Oh, yes, I did." He wiggled the fingers on his right hand. "I hope I didn't break anything."

"You didn't," Isabella said, winking at Grace. "I'm going home now. You'll have to tell me all about your troubles in the morning."

"I'm sure as hell not going to discuss that again," Jack muttered.

"Thank you again," Grace told the woman. "I hope Mac wasn't any trouble."

"He's a good boy," Isabella assured her, pushing open the back door. "Does he belong to Jet?"

Jack answered for her. "I doubt it."

The housekeeper hesitated. "That child has a McLintock look about him. Looks like Jason did when he was that age."

"All babies look alike," Jack muttered.

"Not really," Grace said. She was beginning to realize that Jack McLintock was all bark and no bite. He grouched quite a bit, but he had defended her honor and protected her from a half-drunk cowboy. He'd been quite heroic, even though he would look a little worse for wear for the attempt. "Not all babies have a cleft chin," she added, just to annoy him.

His lips thinned.

"McLintock babies do," Isabella called as she stepped into the night. Grace poured herself a glass of water. She would say good-night, then she would go to her room and crawl into bed. It had been a long day, and tomorrow promised to be even longer.

"She always gets the last word," her host said.

"I'm going to bed."

"So soon?" His tone was sarcastic. "Are you certain we've had enough excitement tonight?"

You'll have to get excited all by yourself, she longed to say. "Unless you have any more brothers I can talk to, I'm going to bed." She set the glass in the sink and moved toward the door.

"Tomorrow," he said, lifting the meat from his face. "We'll get answers tomorrow."

"I'm sure we will," Grace said, though she wasn't sure at all. The brothers were handsome devils whose charming smiles could cover up just about anything.

Even a son.

Grace hurried to her room, unpacked her small bag and used the bathrooom. Mac slept, completely unaware of the questions swirling around him. He was a good baby, patient even with a woman whose only experience with children had been years ago. She'd been a child herself. A child old past her years. A child who had seen too much and whose heart had been broken too many times.

Grace crawled into bed. She'd been smart to bring

her overnight things. Of course, she'd thought she'd be sleeping in a San Antonio hotel tonight. She hadn't counted on a ranch. Or four McLintocks. But despite everything, she'd enjoyed herself. Once she settled Mac, life would return to normal. That would be fine, she assured herself right before falling asleep. Normal was quiet. Normal was peaceful.

Normal was lonely, a voice inside reminded her. She was accustomed to lonely, Grace argued. There were worse things in life.

"HELL, JET, YOU'VE GOT to give me more to go on than that." Jack tapped the copy of the birth certificate. "There's a McLintock name on there, and someone has to be responsible for that little boy."

Jethro poured himself a cup of coffee and eyed his older brother. "You look like hell. What happened last night? Can't hold your liquor?"

"No. Greg Enders couldn't. He made some remarks to our houseguest and I warned him to shut up."

"And he hit you."

"He flapped his mouth again, hit me and I hit him. He was still on the floor when I left the bar." Jack couldn't help the pride that crept into his voice.

"Guess you haven't lost your touch."

Jack drained his coffee mug and leaned forward. "You want to cut the small talk and tell me about Lucy Bagwell?"

Jet stared into his coffee as if the answers were there in the bottom of the cup. "Nothing to tell," he said after a long moment. "The kid isn't mine, though I wouldn't mind too much if he was."

"You've seen him?"

"Not yet."

"Just wait. He looks like Jason did at that age."

"I'm not sure I remember." Jethro sat down across from his brother. "Those years are a blur, and it's not like Ma had a lot of time to take pictures."

"I want the truth, Jet. Are you—is there any chance in hell that you're this boy's father?"

There was a long silence. "We played in a place outside of Dallas a year ago last March. Gus looked it up."

"Do you remember anyone named Lucy?"

"Hell, Jack, that was almost a year and a half ago."

"Fifteen months is not that long."

"It is when you play in a different bar each weekend. You know the schedule we keep—"

"I don't want to hear it, Jet. I just want to know if you slept with anyone that weekend, and if that kid could be yours."

"He's not mine."

"This Grace woman might want blood tests," Jack warned.

"Fine." Jet's gaze didn't waver. Jack held it long enough to make his point, then got up and refilled his coffee cup. His eye was sore, the skin still hot and puffy, but he wasn't in bad shape. He'd almost enjoyed popping that big mouth of Enders. Maybe he wasn't as old as he thought.

"What about Grace?"

She wasn't cut out to deal with drunk and horny cowboys, that was obvious. "What about her?"

"She seemed nice. Pretty, too."

"She's not your type."

Jet looked surprised, then he laughed. "And my type is?"

"Skinny blondes with big attitudes and bigger—"

"Good morning," Grace said, making Jack close his mouth. She stepped into the kitchen, the chubby baby tucked against her hip. The child surveyed the two men and then grinned. "This is Mac," Grace said to Jet.

"Call me *Uncle* Jet," the young man told the wide-eyed baby.

Jack glared at him. "This isn't the time or place to tease."

Jet ignored him. "Where'd that boy get that chin?"

"That's what I'm here to find out," Grace said as Jet stood up and held his arms out to the child.

"Will he come to me?"

"Let's see." She gave Mac a chance to go to Jet, and the boy leaned away from her and into the cowboy's arms.

Jet looked comfortable holding him, but he turned to Jack with a worried expression. "Does Jimmy know about him?"

"No. He's spending the weekend in town while the play is on." Jack saw the likeness right away as Jet and the child were almost at eye level. Now he understood why Grace had given him such a strange look when he'd held Mac yesterday. She'd seen it, and so had Isabella. "Does he have a last name?"

"I guess he's a McLintock now," Jet answered, grinning as the baby patted his face.

"I think Lucy used 'Bagwell,'" Grace said.

Jack got up and poured another cup of coffee, then handed it to Grace. "Here," he said, figuring her for a woman who needed caffeine in the morning. Her grateful expression told him he'd guessed right.

"Thank you." She went to the refrigerator and took out one of the bottles of formula that were stacked neatly on the door. Jack watched as she hid the bottle from the baby's sight while she held it under hot tap water at the sink. Mac hollered the minute he saw Grace wipe it dry with a nearby dish towel.

"I'll take it," Jet offered. He sat down in a chair, stuck the bottle in the baby's mouth and grinned. "I always knew I'd be one heck of a fine uncle."

Jack took a sip of his coffee. "Getting ahead of yourself, aren't you?"

"Hey, he's not mine," Jet said. "But that doesn't mean he isn't ours." He gave his older brother a questioning look. "Are you sure he's not yours?" And this time he didn't smile after he asked the question.

Jack figured that didn't deserve an answer. Grace, looking real pretty in white shorts and a pink T-shirt, brought her coffee cup to the table and sat down.

"Who do I talk to next?"

Jack and Jet looked at each other.

"Jimmy-Joe," Jack said.

"Is he here on the ranch?"

"Not this weekend. Not until tomorrow night."

"He's an actor," Jet explained. He lifted the empty

bottle from Mac's mouth and tilted him into a sitting position. "He's in a show in town. *Paint Your Wagon.*"

Grace looked confused. "Isn't that a movie?"

"It was a play first," Jet said. Mac coughed, and Jet looked at Grace. "Now what?"

"He needs to be burped."

"Oh. Yeah. I forgot."

Jack sighed. Didn't Jet remember how to take care of a baby? "Sit him up a little higher and pat his back."

Jet did as he was told, and the little boy let out a burp that would rival anything heard in the bunkhouse. "Hey, kid, nice going. Jimmy-Joe takes his acting real serious," Jet said after he stopped chuckling. "He's going to Hollywood in a couple of weeks."

One week and six days, Jack thought silently. In less than two weeks they would all go their separate ways. He wondered what it would be like to stand out in the yard and wave goodbye. He wondered if he would wish he was going, too. No, he wouldn't. He would find one of those old plastic lawn chairs, and he would open a beer and sit in the shade and watch the grass grow.

Life would be good, all right.

"Jack?"

He blinked and realized the gray-eyed woman was looking at him as if she was waiting for an answer. "Yeah?"

"Can we go to town and talk to your other brother? I'd like to get Mac settled as soon as possible."

"Settled?" he repeated. "With Jimmy-Joe?" The

woman didn't realize that Jimmy-Joe didn't know the meaning of the word.

"Yes," she said in that soft voice that made him feel like some kind of brute. "The sooner Mac finds his father, the better."

"I don't think—"

"He shouldn't be too hard to track down," Jet said, interrupting his older brother. He grinned at Jack, but Jack sure didn't feel like grinning back. "And I want to be there to see him find out he's a daddy, too."

"This isn't something that needs an audience."

"Well, how about moral support?"

Mac held his arms out to Grace, and she leaned over and scooped him into her lap. "I really don't care how you decide to talk to your brother," Grace informed the two men. "But it needs to be done soon. A child's future is at stake."

She made him feel like the kid in kindergarten who went around telling everyone else that there was no Santa Claus. Still, Jack cleared his throat and tried to explain. "I'm not trying to make things difficult for you," he said. "And I want what's best for the boy, too. It's just that Jimmy-Joe is an actor. He's got some fancy agent in Los Angeles, and he's heading there in a couple of weeks. I don't think he's the man you're looking for." And if he is, Jack added silently, he'd be tied to the barn and made to live up to his responsibilities.

"Don't you think we need to find out as soon as possible?"

"I'm not sure where he's staying," Jack hedged. J.J.'s womanizing was legendary, and there was no telling where he'd slept last night. And Jack wasn't going to start calling various Locklin women to ask, either.

"We have tickets to the show tonight. Grace can have mine, since I've got a gig."

Jack tore his gaze away from the brown-eyed baby and looked over at Jet. He was getting pretty damned tired of his brother's suggestions. "I thought you were going to see the first half."

Jet shrugged. "I went to the dress rehearsal on Thursday and saw the whole thing. Didn't know Jimmy-Joe could sing that well."

Grace looked uncertain. "I can't take Mac to the show."

"One of Isabella's daughters can watch him. Lord knows we have enough people around here to take care of one more child." He might as well tell the woman what she wanted to hear, and that was she would get her chance to talk to another McLintock.

"Yes," Grace said. "That's exactly what I've been thinking, too."

Anxious to escape, Jack stood up. "I've got work to do. Guess I'd better get at it." He nodded at Isabella, who had entered the kitchen to start cleaning up the breakfast dishes.

"Take Grace with you," Jet said. "I'll bet you've never been on a ranch, have you, Grace?"

"No, but—"

Isabella patted Mac's head. "I'll take the boy. We'll go visit Lina for a little while. The girls will love playing with him."

Jack knew when he was being backed into a corner. "I'll be out back. You might want to change. That is, if you've brought clothes fit for a ranch." He hoped she hadn't.

"I have jeans," she said. "Is that all right?"

"Yeah."

"I'll wait for you," Jet offered. "Jack has to see if he can get the truck started."

"All right," she said in that soft voice that did funny things to Jack's heart. He left the kitchen, jamming his hat on his head as he made his escape. A woman had no business here on the ranch, and neither did a baby. There was no room for either one, not on his ranch or in his life. He was through with all that, but Jimmy-Joe might not be. Jack took a deep breath of the humid morning air and hurried to the barn. He hated to think that his younger brother's dreams were about to be postponed or, at the very least, complicated beyond belief, but that's what happened when a man didn't think past what hung between his thighs.

OKAY, SHE SHOULDN'T BE having fun. Grace knew she should be back in Dallas where she belonged. Her compact apartment held a desk piled high with work; she had deadlines for two computer programs and their manuals and one more waiting as soon as she signed the contract. Her job was to explain the unexplainable, at least in layman's terms. What she couldn't explain was why she didn't mind staying another day—and yes, another night—on the McLintock ranch.

She could leave. She could take the child home with

her, let the lawyers decide what to do with Mac. But then Mac's future would be out of her hands; her promise to deliver Mac to his father would have gone unfulfilled. Lucy deserved better than that.

And so did Mac. So Grace handed Mac into Isabella's plump embrace, changed into her jeans and prepared to tour the ranch. With a handsome cowboy, of course.

Lucy wouldn't believe it.

"IT'S THE ANSWER to everything," Jet said, following Isabella to the clothesline. He set the heavy basket of wet clothes at her feet. "Don't you think?"

She shook her head and reached into the basket. "You always had such an imagination, Jethro. Ever since you were a little boy."

"But it's simple," he said, stepping back to avoid a flapping shirtsleeve. "We've all been worried about Jack, and now here comes a beautiful woman, right to the front door. It's clear he likes her."

"And how do you figure that?"

"He danced with her last night at the Stampede." To Jet it was simple. Jack had held a woman in his arms. Jack had danced with her, defended her honor, brought her back to the ranch and installed her in a spare room. Once there was a woman on the ranch, well, hell. Anything could happen.

Isabella's eyebrows rose. "You think that is a sign?"

"Yeah, I do. If we play our cards right." If nothing was left to chance. "If Grace stays, if she and Jack get, uh, together, that means that Jack won't be alone when we leave. He'll have Grace and the baby."

"Maybe he *wants* to be alone," the old woman pointed out. "Maybe he is looking forward to being on his own, too, just the way the rest of you are."

Jet shook his head. "I don't believe that for a minute. I think he's putting on a good show so the rest of us don't feel bad about leaving."

Isabella shrugged and reached for another shirt. "You can't make two people fall in love, Jet."

"I do it all the time." He shoved the bag of clothespins farther along the line so she could reach them. "I sing the songs and they get closer together and pretty soon they're rubbing against each other and he's whispering in her ear and she—"

"Stop it," Isabella laughed. "I don't want to hear any more of your nonsense."

"It's not nonsense," he protested, his feelings injured.

"Then you are going to sing to Jack and Grace?" She waved toward the west. "They are a mile away by now. I don't think they're going to hear you."

"Very funny. I hope that mule gets loose again and takes down the clothesline."

"No, you don't. You lost two shirts last time."

Jet shrugged. "They were old."

"You carried on for hours about having to spend money buying new ones," she reminded him. "Tell me, Jet, what are you going to do about the baby?"

"Where is he?"

"Lina and the girls are fussing over him while I get

the clothes hung out. Everyone loves a baby. No matter who he belongs to."

"He's not mine, Bella."

"I know that, but you should talk to Jack and tell him why. And maybe you should talk to Jimmy, too. That little boy is a McLintock. Anyone with eyes can see that."

"Yeah. Jimmy has a lot to answer for. Or Jason. I guess he's no saint, either."

Isabella stopped working and put her hands on her hips. "I raised that boy better than that. He's not the kind to hang around bars and pick up women."

"Are you saying that I am?"

"It's your life-style. Not Jason's."

"I don't take chances. And I don't have as many women as you all like to think I do."

Isabella shrugged. "Maybe. Maybe not. But Jason isn't like you. Once he gives his heart, he will give it forever. And I don't think he'll sleep with the girls just to have a good time."

Jet sure as hell didn't want to discuss his sex life with the woman who had practically raised him since he was ten. "I thought we were talking about Jack's love life."

"You were. I am talking about the child. He belongs here, to one of you. And one of you must raise him."

"Exactly. And Jack is the perfect one to do it, too. He raised all of us, and he did a pretty good job."

"He may not want to. He is buying some new cattle, hiring some new cowhands, talking about going fishing in Montana. He does not talk about women and babies and becoming a father."

"He'll get used to the idea," Jet declared. "I think we all have to help him."

"Not me," the woman said. "I am minding my own business."

"Since when?"

"Since I decided to retire and sit in the shade and watch the grandbabies play," she said.

"Yeah, right." He didn't believe the retiring talk for a minute. Jet adjusted the brim of his hat and looked toward the west. "Jack likes this woman. All I'm saying is that we ought to give him some help."

"You have work to do," Isabella reminded him. "Unless you want to help me hang clothes?"

Jet backed up. "Think I'll ride over to the east pasture and see if everything's all right." He left the old cook shaking her head, but he wasn't about to let her comments bother him. She knew as well as he did that Jack wasn't going to know what to do with himself once the brothers went their separate ways. Once the money was distributed and they were all free, things would never be the same.

Which would make a good song title. "Never the Same Again." He liked it. Jet began to whistle, which set the birds flying off the electrical wires as he walked by.

HE HAD GIVEN HER A HAT. Battered, with an odor of sweat rimming the dark-edged inner band, it wasn't a great-looking Stetson, but Grace wasn't about to complain. In fact, she thought it gave her a certain cowgirl flair. It also protected her face from the sun that already blasted the Texas landscape.

And there was lots of landscape. For a couple of hours, Grace obediently looked in whatever direction Jack pointed. She admired the red-and-white cattle, smiled at the sight of the calves frolicking across the pastures and squinted at the brand, until she realized that what looked like an *M* with an extra flip was actually an *ML* stuck together. She tried to remain remote, but it wasn't easy, especially since she'd never been on a cattle ranch until now. "How many cattle do you have here?"

"Hundreds" was the clipped answer. "'Course, there are more now, with the calves," he added, shifting the truck into a higher gear. Grace braced herself by holding on to the dashboard as they bounced over the rutted dirt road.

"This is a big ranch. I don't have to see it all in one day," she managed to say between bounces.

"You couldn't," he replied, glancing at her. "The truck doesn't hold that much gas."

"Oh." Grace looked around at rolling fields topped with a cloudless blue sky. She took a deep breath and felt worlds away from Dallas. She'd almost forgotten what it was like to be without Mac. She'd cared for him for the past couple of weeks, while Lucy was in the hospital, and, though she'd grown to adore the chubby child, it felt good to be free from worrying that she was doing the right thing for him twenty-four hours a day.

"You've never been out on a ranch before?"

"No," she admitted. "I'm pretty much a city girl."

"Yeah? You grow up in Dallas?"

Grace hesitated. She didn't like discussing her personal life, especially not with strangers. "Pretty much," she replied. "What about you?"

"I've lived here all my life," Jack said.

"On this ranch?"

"Yep. The four of us have never lived anywhere else, except for when Jason went to college."

"You're very lucky. Not many people have that kind of stability."

He chuckled. "Growing up around here wasn't what you'd call 'stable,' lady. We worked our butts off trying to keep this place going."

"And it looks as if you succeeded."

"Eventually," he admitted, slowing the truck as they came to a muddy stream. "For now."

"That's all I want for Mac, that kind of stable life," she said. "That's all Lucy wanted, too, was for her child to be raised with his family."

"And if he's not a McLintock? What then?" He stopped the truck, turned off the engine and turned to look at her.

"I don't know. I never thought the birth certificate would be wrong."

He looked as if he felt sorry for her. "Honey, people lie all the time."

She met his gaze. "Exactly."

"No one here is lying to you."

She raised her eyebrows. "No?"

"No."

"If he doesn't belong here, I'll take him back to Dallas with me. I'll make sure he has a family who loves him, and I'll see that he is happy and safe." She paused, then added, "But there's nothing that makes me believe he *doesn't* belong here."

Jack McLintock's gaze didn't waver. "And there's nothing that makes me believe he does."

"I guess we have our work cut out for us, then," she said, wishing he would stop looking at her as if she was out to con the entire family.

"Yeah," he agreed, "I guess we do." He looked away and turned the key in the ignition. "Guess we'd better head back. It'll be lunchtime soon, and I wouldn't want to be accused of starving the city folk."

Grace grabbed the dashboard again as Jack backed up the truck, then headed back the way they came. He'd been honest with her. That was more than she'd expected, especially after last night and Jet's denial of fatherhood.

Not that she was going to trust any of these McLintock men, of course. It was her job to find out the truth and deal with it. If these cowboys thought that she was easily fooled, a person who could be conned into believing anything and everything they said, well, they were wrong.

Grace Daniels was nobody's fool.

4

"THANK YOU FOR SHOWING me around." The truck bounced to a stop in front of a weathered barn where a couple of curious horses lifted their heads and looked over the corral fence toward them.

"You're welcome." He almost smiled. "It was safer than taking you back to the Stampede."

"I had a good time last night. Until the fight, that is." Grace opened the door and, grateful to have made it back to the ranch with all of her bones still connected, stepped out. She looked at the horses and wondered if touring on horseback would have been easier.

"Do you ride?" he said, coming around the front of the truck.

"No." Riding horses was another one of those dreams that she'd shelved, along with Thanksgiving dinner at Grandmother's house and teenage sleepover parties.

"How can you be a Texan and not know how to ride a horse?" he teased.

Grace tried to keep her tone light. "Didn't I tell you I was a city girl?"

"I guess you did," he drawled, but as she turned to go back to the house he touched her shoulder. "Look, Grace, we might have gotten off on the wrong foot, and

I take my share of responsibility for that. But you could have given the family some warning before you came driving up with a baby and a birth certificate. You can't blame a man for being surprised or for trying to defend himself. We're not so bad," he said, looking down at her. "If it weren't for Mac, you might even like us a little."

"I can blame a man who doesn't take care of his child."

"And if he didn't know the child existed?"

"Lucy spoke as if he knew."

"You're sure about that?"

Grace paused. "Not exactly. It was just an impression I had."

"Pretty big impression," he pointed out.

"And raising Mac is a pretty big responsibility. The right person ought to do it."

"And that is?"

"His father. Or a loving adoptive family."

Jack frowned. "Strangers?"

"Adoption is a wonderful alternative." *Adoption* was a magic word, another dream that had never happened.

"Then, why don't you adopt him yourself?"

"It's not that easy." She shoved her hands in her pockets and gazed at the horses. "I wish it was, but it's not."

"It might be easier than finding Mac's father," he pointed out.

"Meaning it might be easier for one of your brothers if Mac was adopted by someone else."

"That's not what I meant."

"I'll find Mac's father, no matter who he is," Grace said. "I made a promise and I intend to keep it."

Jack started to say something, but then looked as if he'd changed his mind. "Have Isabella fix you some lunch. Tell her I'll get my own later."

Grace watched him walk toward the barn. She would talk to his brother tonight, and they would decide what would be done about Mac. Jimmy-Joe the actor would have attracted Lucy, especially if he was as good-looking as the other men in the family. Jason, the young college graduate, would have been too young for her neighbor. But then again, it was hard to tell. It wasn't up to her to decide which brother was Mac's father—Jack was taking care of that. It was simply up to her to deliver the baby when his father was identified. Getting more involved with the family wasn't part of the plan.

And Grace always followed the plan. She'd learned a long time ago that everything was easier with a plan. And her plan right now included leaving the ranch tomorrow. By tomorrow she certainly should know more about Mac's parentage and what to do next. He belonged with his own flesh and blood, if possible. That's what Lucy had wanted. That's what Grace had promised.

She returned to the house, and Isabella showed her where Mac was playing. She collected the baby from Isabella's giggling granddaughters and thanked them for watching them. She met Lina, a quiet woman with a shy smile and short dark hair, on the steps of a small white house a few hundred yards from the main house.

"Bring him anytime tonight," she offered. "The girls and I will take care of him while you are at the show."

"Thank you." She balanced the baby on her hip and winced as he tugged a lock of her hair. "I appreciate the help."

"Mom told us about his mother." The young woman reached out and stroked the baby's soft arm. "He will be all right now, I'm sure."

"If I can find his father."

"You will." Lina smiled. "Who would not want such a beautiful son?"

Grace could think of two particular men. "I hope you're right."

"The McLintocks are good men. They will see that he is taken care of."

"Well, I hope so. That's why we're here." She shifted the baby's weight on her hip and unwound her hair from his grip. "Come on, Mac. You look like you need a bath."

"The girls tried to feed him," Lina said, handing Grace a half-empty bottle. "I think he was too interested in everything going on around him to bother with lunch." Lina smiled again. "Don't worry. My mother says that Mac belongs here, and she's never wrong."

"Thanks," Grace said. "I'll keep that in mind."

"TELL HER WE HAVE to leave here at six-thirty." Jack moved through the kitchen and into the living room, Isabella following him as best she could.

"Tell Grace?"

He sighed. "Yeah. Since she's so all-fired anxious to see Jimmy in action, she can be ready on time."

"You were late for dinner," she pointed out. "We ate without you."

"Not the first time." He walked swiftly down the hall and turned the corner toward his bedroom, with Isabella right behind him. When he reached his door, he stopped. "Bella, what are you doing?"

"I want to talk to you," she said, poking him in the chest with one plump finger.

"I'm about talked out." Between Grace and Jet, Jack had just about all he could stand. "Can this wait?"

"No."

He leaned in the doorway of his room and prayed for patience. He was hot, tired and hungry. He had to clean up to go to town. He had to sit through another one of Jimmy-Joe's plays, and then he had to find out if the boy had been making time with some Dallas woman last year. All the while he'd have Grace hanging on every word, her very attractive little body distracting him every time she moved. She was lovely, but she didn't belong on the ranch. She needed to leave before he forgot what cows were. Before he forgot that he didn't have the energy for pursuing beautiful women. Or the money.

"The child doesn't belong to Jet and he doesn't belong to you. Which leaves Jimmy."

Jack folded his arms across his chest. "Not necessarily. Jimmy has more sense and less time than Jet. I don't think Jet would lie to me, but then again, I don't think he remembers all the women he, uh, meets."

"Men." Isabella rolled her eyes. "Don't you remember when Jet was so sick with the mumps?"

"He missed out on a pretty good fishing trip."

"He was fourteen. And his private parts swelled up like watermelons."

Jack hid a grin. He'd forgotten about that. Jet hadn't known whether to be embarrassed or proud. "And?"

"Mumps can cause sterility."

"You're saying *Jet* can't have children?"

"I'm saying you should talk to him before you jump to any conclusions, that's all." She looked as if she wanted to say something else.

"And?" he urged. "I assume there's more you have on your mind."

"The young lady is very pretty. And very kind."

"Which has nothing to do with me," he pointed out. "Nothing at all," he felt obliged to repeat.

"When's the last time you were with a woman?"

"That is none of your business." There was no way in hell he was going to admit that it had been well over a year. Before the librarian had moved to San Antonio, though. Come to think of it, he hadn't had much time to read, either.

The cook sniffed. "Everything around here turns out to be my business sooner or later. I think *you* should think about taking advantage of having a lovely woman in your home."

"Seduce the houseguest? I don't think so."

Isabella shot him a disgusted look. "I am not talking about seduction. I'm talking about enjoying a woman's company. For once."

"I'll 'enjoy' when and where I damn please," Jack sputtered. With that said, he turned around and shut his bedroom door. Privacy was all he asked for, and there was little of it here. But that was going to change. In one week and six days.

He stripped off his shirt and headed for the bathroom he shared with Jet. Seduction wasn't a bad idea. In fact, he was planning to look around and start dating. He would have the time and the money and, hell, even the energy. He would be free to sample the pleasures of San Antonio, look up the librarian, flirt with pretty ladies who gave him an interested smile. Once he paid off the mortgages on the ranch, he might be free to sow some long overdue wild oats. Or at least sleep at night without wondering if he would be able to pay the real estate taxes.

Jack leaned forward and examined his face in the mirror. He hoped he wasn't too old to have fun.

He hoped he still remembered what it was.

SHE'D FORGOTTEN MOST of the story, but remembered that Lee Marvin had played the experienced gold miner in the movie. Jimmy-Joe McLintock—Jim McLock on the program—was the younger farmer, accidentally involved in the discovery of gold and eventually in love with the wife of the older miner. Jimmy-Joe had an easy singing style, but his deep voice and impressive stage presence made him look like a star.

And Grace had no doubt that Jimmy-Joe McLintock was going places.

He was taller than Jet and not as heavily muscled as Jack. Or so Grace guessed. She watched in fascination as the first act ended and the crowd erupted in cheers for Jimmy and the others.

"Well?" Jack turned to her as the lights went on for intermission. He'd rolled up the paper program as if he was going to hit someone with it. "What did you think?"

"It's a good show. I love the music." She didn't know what to say about the third McLintock brother. He looked like the kind of man who would have women dropping at his feet. Lucy would have loved him. And probably had.

Isabella struggled to her feet and, her enormous purse hanging over her arm, fanned herself with her program. "I'm going outside to get some air."

Jack rose. "We'll join you in a few minutes."

Grace fanned herself with her program and stood, too. The crowd was hurrying outside, presumably toward the bar that was set up on the front lawn of the old theater. She'd worn the sundress she'd worn yesterday, but even the lightweight cotton fabric felt uncomfortably hot against her skin. Jack wore a short-sleeved white shirt and beige slacks, but for some reason he still looked like a cowboy.

"I'll buy you a drink," the rancher said, touching her elbow to guide her out of her seat and up the aisle. "I think we could both use something cold."

She sipped iced tea from a plastic cup while Jack settled for something with bourbon and ice. They stood on the shaded side of the building and sipped their drinks. Isabella was nowhere to be seen, but several people smiled at Jack and gave Grace a curious look. A short, stocky man hurried over to Jack and shook his hand.

"Two weeks to go, huh, son? I expect you'll be sowing your own wild oats afterward." He looked down at Grace and grinned, his face red from the heat. "And who is this lovely lady?"

Grace held out her hand and the man held it. "I'm Grace Daniels. A...family friend."

Jack cleared his throat. "The man who is holding your hand is Harry White, vice president of the only bank in town."

"Yes, ma'am," Harry said, finally releasing her hand. "I'm right pleased to meet you. I'll bet you're here for the festivities."

"Festivities? You mean Jason's party?"

"That's right, among other things." He winked at Jack. "A big time ahead for all of the McLintocks, right, son?"

"Yeah," Jack muttered. "A big time."

"Heard Jet's heading to Nashville." Harry took out a kerchief and wiped his brow.

"That's what he says."

"Well, you tell him that the Whites will buy all of his records. Janie can't wait to hear him on the radio someday."

"Thanks, Harry. I'll tell him."

"Nice meeting you, Miz Daniels," the banker said. "See you at the party!"

"It was nice meeting you, too," Grace managed to say before the little man disappeared into the crowd.

"You're supposed to be a cousin," Jack said.

"I forgot. I just went blank."

"Well," he drawled, "that I can believe, all right. You wouldn't make a very good spy. Otherwise you wouldn't have driven into the middle of my property claiming to have brought me my son. You would have checked us out first, I think."

Grace bit back a laugh. "I guess you have a point. I *could* have been sneakier, I suppose, but I never thought that Mac's father didn't know he existed." She looked at her watch. "I hope Lina didn't have any trouble putting him to bed. He had such an exciting day."

"Did you know his mother well?"

"She was my neighbor. I didn't know her until she moved into the apartment next to mine. She was very pregnant at the time, and we became friends after she had Mac. I didn't know she was sick."

He took a sip of his drink. "What happened?"

"She'd refused to have any treatment that would endanger her pregnancy. It ended up costing her her life."

"I'm sorry," he said. "She must have been a very brave person."

"She was. And she was funny, too. Even when she was suffering, she wouldn't let anyone feel sorry for her."

The bell rang to announce the end of intermission, so

Grace and Jack walked with the crowd back to the theater. Jack remained silent long after they had tossed their empty cups into the trash bin and taken their seats in the fifth row from the front. Isabella was already in her seat, and she smiled at them as they sat down.

"You are having fun?" she whispered as the lights dimmed.

"Yes. Very much."

"Good," the older woman said. And the curtains opened on the second half of the show.

Fun, Grace thought, was all relative. She'd never thought that delivering Mac to his father would be classed as "fun." She hadn't intended to have fun when she came to the ranch. She'd intended to do what she had to do and then leave. Since arriving in Locklin, she'd danced in a country-western bar, ridden in a pickup truck, eaten green chili, and now sat watching the Locklin Playhouse version of *Paint Your Wagon*. With Mac's father as one of the stars?

She would know in another hour or two. Unless someone was lying.

JIMMY-JOE HAD BETTER not lie to him. None of the boys had pulled that in years, not since they'd left elementary school. And there was Grace, who would be listening to every word. He wondered if he could figure out a way to get her to stand quietly off to one side while he handled Jimmy. Yeah, right. Grace would be right in the middle of it. He had to admire her devotion to the baby, but he sure as hell wished she would let him handle this his own way.

Which would be in private. He managed to squeeze through the crowd backstage until he reached the center of attention. As usual, there was Jimmy, his makeup still on, his shirt unbuttoned and a grin a mile wide on his handsome mug. A couple of real pretty women clustered around him, which explained Jimmy's satisfied smile. Jack didn't know how his brothers found the time to romance women, between their ranch work and their careers.

"Hey, Jack!" Jimmy waved when he saw him approach. "How'd you like the show?"

"Great," he managed to say, moving sideways to avoid a couple of men covered in makeup and holding full champagne glasses.

"Act 2 might have been a little slow," Jimmy said as Jack shook his hand. "Could you tell I missed a line near the end?"

"Not at all. The show was great."

"Thanks. What happened to your eye?"

"I got into a fight with Greg Enders at the Stampede last night."

Jimmy burst into laughter. "No, really, what happened to your eye?"

Jack sighed. "Never mind. But I got in the last punch."

His younger brother grinned, then looked past Jack. "Did you bring a date?"

"Well, not exactly." He reached over and helped

Grace make a hole through the crowd. "This is Grace. She's visiting us for the weekend."

"Really? Nice to meet you!"

"I enjoyed the show," she said, raising her voice over the sound of celebrating actors. "You were wonderful."

"Thanks, Grace." He almost looked as if he was blushing, but Jack was sure that was the stage makeup. "Are you two coming to the party at Nellie's afterward?"

"No, but I need to talk to you tonight, because—"

"Jimmy!" A pretty blond woman threw her arms around Jimmy and kissed his cheek. "I *loved* the show! I couldn't take my *eyes* off you!"

"Thanks, Chrissy." He put his arm around her waist. "Darlin', meet my brother Jack and his girlfriend Grace."

"Hi, y'all. Isn't Jimmy here just the *greatest?*"

Jack ignored the "girlfriend" comment. "Yeah. The greatest." He looked at Jimmy. "Are you coming home tonight?"

"I wasn't planning on it," he admitted. "But I can be home first thing in the morning."

"Good enough," Jack agreed. He wasn't about to discuss illegitimate children in the middle of the backstage chaos, and he wasn't sure that Jimmy's dressing room would be any more private.

Grace tugged on his arm. "Couldn't we find a place to talk now? I really need to get back to Dallas. My work—"

"Just a minute," he told her, then turned to Jimmy. "You have a minute?"

Jimmy's smile died, and he unwound the little blonde's clinging arms from around his neck. "What's the matter, Jack?"

"Nothing that can't wait," Jack said, realizing a bit guiltily that he was going to spoil Jimmy's big evening. He had been so damned careful to avoid any discussions before the show that he hadn't thought about ruining the fun afterward. He should have realized that the cast would be in a state of euphoria after the curtain had come down. "I'll see you in the morning."

"But—" Grace sputtered.

"Later," he told her, gently moving her backward and out of Jimmy's hearing. "We don't have to do this now."

"But of course we do," she insisted. "I can't take any more time away from my work. Tomorrow's Sunday and I need to be home."

"You'll be on your way soon enough," he told her, taking her elbow and hustling her out of the backstage area toward the stairs. "Jimmy will be home in the morning. We can talk to him then. I don't know why I let you talk me into doing this now."

"Because I can't stay here forever, that's why. I have to get back to work. I have projects to—"

"Lady, your work schedule is the last thing I'm thinking about right now." They were outside and alone at the side of the theater. "I've been letting you call the shots here, and now that's going to stop. I've got a black eye and—"

"You like it," she said, lifting her chin to meet his gaze. "Don't expect me to feel sorry for you. You didn't mind punching that other cowboy at all."

"That's not the point." He hid his smile, remembering the surprised expression on Enders's big mug as his fist connected with flesh and bone. "I'm not ruining Jimmy's big night tonight. I'm not changing my life around because some city woman thinks one of us is the father of that child. I've got things to do, and I'm not getting them done."

"Like what?"

"What?"

"What *things* are you not getting done? What *things* are more important than finding Mac's father?"

"For all I know, Mac's father is some bartender in Dallas who thought it was funny to make up a name one night. For all I know you have no business on my ranch." That seemed to shut her up. "I'm a busy man. With a business to run. And I'm getting ready to give one hell of a party. Jason turns twenty-one, remember? And that birthday means a lot more than blowing out a few candles." He wasn't about to explain the trust fund to a stranger. Lord knows she didn't need any more reasons to think that one of the boys would make a great father. A rich father.

"Look," she said, keeping up with him as he strode down the sidewalk to the parked truck. "I don't care about your birthday party. I care about Mac. And I want to know that he is safe, with his father, before I leave. Why do I have to keep saying this over and over again?"

"You're asking a lot, lady." Jack began to lose his temper. "You can't just come into Locklin and start pointing fingers at people, saying, 'Are you a daddy?'"

He opened the door of his old Cadillac and motioned for her to get in.

She did, and Jack caught a glimpse of shapely legs before the flowered dress was smoothed into place. "You don't have to yell," she said.

He walked around the car to the driver's side and counted to ten. Yell? She hadn't heard him yell. Not yet. He was still using his calm voice, damn it all to hell. Jack slid behind the wheel and slammed the door shut with more force than he intended. Grace jumped a little and put on her seat belt. "I'm not yelling."

"*If* you're telling the truth, then Jimmy-Joe or Jethro is Mac's father. I think Jason is too young. Lucy never talked about her boyfriend being younger than she was."

"Which might let Jimmy and Jet off the hook?" he asked as he put the car in gear and headed home.

"No. They both look older. And Lucy was in her late thirties, I think. It was hard to tell, because she'd had a pretty hard life."

He sighed. "Great. Lucy was a hard-living woman with an eye for cowboys. Jet and Jimmy were hard-living cowboys with an eye for women. That doesn't mean any of them actually got together."

Grace gave him a who-do-you-think-you're-kidding look. "Which brings us back to the matter of Mac's chin."

He didn't answer. In fact, he didn't feel like talking

for quite a few miles. He thought he might not talk until tomorrow. Or maybe not until August. In two weeks he would have paid off the ranch. The place would finally be his, without threats from the bank.

He told himself it was foolish to worry about one small woman and one chubby baby. Everything would work out. Jimmy-Joe, the only candidate for daddy now, would take responsibility for his son. Everything else would go along as planned, including the party. Including the distribution of the trust fund money. Little Mac could afford those fancy diapers with the cartoon characters on them. Hell, he could have his own horse and a fancy Hollywood nanny. Jack turned onto the ranch road and headed toward the house. There were lights on; Isabella had arrived home before them.

"I hoped to do this without lawyers and blood tests," Grace said into the darkness. "You're not making this easy."

"Easy?" he repeated. "What in hell is easy about any of this?"

"You don't have to start yelling again."

"I'm not—" He stopped and made a conscious effort to lower his voice. "I'm not yelling," he said once again. He parked the Cadillac beside Grace's Ford, then shut off the engine. He turned to Grace and met her gaze. "I don't need this in my life right now."

"And you think *I* do?"

"Why on earth are you involved? Surely there were authorities—"

"No way," she interrupted. "Not if I could help it. I spent most of my life in foster homes, and I don't want to see Mac in the same situation. He has a chance to grow up with a family, and I'm not going to let anyone take that away from him."

"Growing up in this family might not be the best thing for him. Have you thought of that?"

"Not yet."

"You might give it some thought," he said, his voice quiet.

"You're all flirts," she whispered. "Real charmers."

"Yeah," he said, reaching out to pull her into his arms. "I know." He touched her lips with a gentle kiss, enough pressure for her to know that she was being kissed, but not enough to scare her. He didn't want to part her lips and touch her tongue. He didn't want passion; he merely wanted her to know that she should go back to Dallas before she got into trouble.

But her lips were sweet. And warm. And incredibly soft. He inhaled the light scent of flowers and drew her closer into his arms. She didn't pull away, but she didn't move into his arms, either. She let him kiss her, returning the kiss slightly but almost with more curiosity than passion.

He lifted his head and looked down at her. "Maybe you'd be better off in Dallas."

"Maybe *you* would," she said, her gray eyes large in the dim light. "But I'm not going anywhere."

"That's what I was afraid of," he muttered, releasing her from his arms. "But you can't blame a man for trying."

"I don't blame you for anything," she said, and got out of the car. "You're the kind of man who would tell the truth, no matter what." She turned around and walked to the house without waiting for him to follow. And of course he didn't follow her at all. He stuck his hands in his pockets and looked up at the moon.

He was the kind of man who told the truth, all right. But he was also the kind of man who wanted nothing more than to follow his houseguest to her bed and make love to her.

5

GOOD HEAVENS, WHEN WAS the last time she'd been kissed?

This really was becoming more complicated than she wanted to admit. She thanked Lina's daughter for baby-sitting, paid her enough to make the teenager smile with surprise, and then shut the bedroom door. And locked it, just to make sure. Not that she thought that the oldest McLintock would force himself into her bedroom. He wasn't that kind of man, and it hadn't been that kind of kiss. She didn't know exactly what kind of kiss it was, but it hadn't been threatening. It had been...intriguing. And exciting.

And something to forget as quickly as possible.

Grace tiptoed over to Mac's bed and adjusted his blankets with a careful motion. Thank goodness he slept through the night, though he awoke at sunrise hungry and wanting company. Good thing she was a morning person and liked to see the sun come up.

Mac slept, oblivious to the questions surrounding his future. Grace wondered if she was any closer to finding the baby a home. She could take him back to Dallas, but would that be fair? He had a chance to grow up on a ranch, to know his relatives, to take his rightful place in the family. If she packed up the car in the morning and returned to Dallas, she would be depriving Mac of the chance to be a McLintock. Jack had warned her that none of them would make good fathers, but she wasn't so sure. Nothing she'd seen so far made her doubt her decision to come to Locklin.

If she continued to do what was best for Mac, how could she go wrong? Unless she kept kissing charming cowboys, of course. That part could never happen again. She was too smart to make the same mistake as Lucy.

"ALL I WANT TO KNOW is did you have an affair—or something like that—with a woman named Lucy Bagwell?"

Jimmy eyed his older brother warily. "Jack, it's six-thirty in the morning, and I've had two hours' sleep, and even though it's Sunday you've probably got a list of chores for me to do that are gonna take till sunset, and you're asking me about who I've slept with?"

"Yes." Jimmy's moaning and groaning didn't affect him in the least. "And I want an answer." He'd been up for an hour. When he'd heard Jimmy's truck in the drive, he'd headed for the back porch. They would have privacy out there even if Isabella decided to get up early or Grace had to feed the boy.

Jimmy sat down in one of the plastic lawn chairs and closed his eyes. "Lord, that was one hell of a party."

"Jimmy—"

"And I don't know anyone named Lucy. Can I go to bed now? If I could get two more hours' sleep I—"

"Were you anywhere near Dallas a year ago last March?"

"You and I went to the stock show, remember?"

"A *year* ago last March."

Jimmy frowned and opened his eyes. "Why are you asking?"

"Because Lucy Bagwell had a baby boy. He's six months old, and he's sleeping in the spare room waiting for someone to figure out who his father is."

"And you think he's *mine?*"

"It's sure looking that way."

Jimmy groaned and closed his eyes again. "I can't believe this. What does this Lucy woman want?"

"Could the baby be yours?"

"I don't know. I doubt it. I'm pretty damn careful."

"You don't remember where you were that March? Supposedly she met a McLintock in a bar outside of Dallas and they had a brief affair."

"Maybe if I see her I'll remember. What does she look like?"

Jack hesitated. He knew Jimmy was going to feel even worse when he heard what was coming next. "She's dead. The woman you met last night—Grace— was her neighbor. She promised Lucy to take the baby to his father."

"Which is supposed to be me," Jimmy said, sitting up straight and staring at his brother. "You think I'm a *father?*"

"It's not me and it's not Jet. And Jason isn't home to ask, though I think he's a little young for side trips to Dallas bars."

Jimmy shrugged. "The rest of us managed to get to Dallas when we were that age."

"I can't picture Jason, though."

"No—" Jimmy sighed "—neither can I." He brightened. "Hey, I'm a father! I don't think I'm gonna mind too much."

"You can't take a baby to Hollywood," Jack pointed out.

"Sure I can. I'll take Isabella with me and we'll manage just fine."

"Isabella isn't going to leave her family to go traipsing off to California."

Jimmy's face fell. "The little guy doesn't have anybody but me, does he."

Jack told him the truth, or as much of it as he knew. "Not that I know of. If you're his father. The name on the birth certificate just gave the first initial of J, so that could be any one of us. Or else the name on the birth certificate isn't the correct one."

"Sure it is," Grace said, opening the screen door and stepping onto the porch. The little boy was tucked against her hip, and he looked at both men and smiled. "That's why Lucy named him Mac. She said he should have his father's name."

"Hey," Jimmy said, staring at the boy. "So you're the little guy we've been talking about."

Mac held out his arms, and Grace let him go to the young man. "I guess he wants to say hello," Grace said.

"He sure looks like a McLintock," Jimmy said, holding the baby on his lap and looking at his face. "But I don't remember anyone named Lucy."

"She was a tall redhead with blue eyes," Grace said. "She had a low, raspy voice and a big laugh."

"I've, uh, never exactly been attracted to redheads," he admitted, looking embarrassed. "I think I would have remembered." He turned to Jack, a hopeful expression on his face. "Jethro likes redheads. Remember the waitress over in El Paso that came all the way out here to—"

"Never mind," Jack said, cutting him off. He didn't think Grace needed to hear the details of his brothers' exploits with women. "I've got my reasons to believe that this little boy isn't Jet's."

"What do you mean?"

Jack shook his head, hoping Jimmy would get the message. He wasn't going to discuss Jet's experience with mumps while Grace was listening.

Jimmy bounced the baby on his knee, and the child gurgled as if he was enjoying it. "And he's not yours, Jack?"

"No." If he was, he'd know it. He'd sure as hell remember having sex with someone. It wasn't something he got to do every day. Or night. He avoided looking at Grace. She hadn't said anything to him yet, probably figuring he was some kind of oversexed Texas stud who spent his evenings groping women inside his old Cadillac.

"Can I get anyone coffee?" Grace asked.

Jack frowned. "You don't have to wait on us."

"I was trying to be helpful," she said, meeting his

gaze. "I thought we could sit here like civilized people and discuss Mac's future."

"You know," Jimmy said, a puzzled expression on his face, "I don't—"

"Coffee, then," Jack said, ignoring his brother. Grace was wearing those shorts again and that knit shirt that showed off some tempting curves. He wondered why she wasn't married. "We'll all have coffee."

Jimmy tried again. "I have to check—"

"Black, right?" Grace asked.

"Right."

Jimmy stood up and plopped the baby in Jack's lap. "You take him for a sec. I have to see something."

"Hey," Jack said, gripping the child securely. "Where are you going?"

"I'll be back," he called, the screen door banging shut behind him. Jack looked down at the baby, who eyed him with a solemn expression. "Hey, kid. Remember me? Uncle Jack. That's not so bad, is it?" The child continued to stare at him, so Jack tried the bouncing-knee trick, but Mac still stared up at him until Grace stepped outside. She carried two steaming mugs and set them down on the old pine table that was shoved up against the outside wall of the house.

"Jimmy said he'd get his own," she said, explaining the two cups. She left him alone on the porch once again, and in a few minutes returned with a streamlined version of a stroller. "You don't have to hold him. He likes his stroller." She lifted Mac out of Jack's lap. Jack noticed she was careful not to touch him. He told himself he wasn't disappointed.

He watched as she settled Mac into his stroller, adjusted the safety straps and fixed it so he could look at both of them while they talked.

"I guess we've found Mac's father," she said.

"I guess so." Though he wasn't completely convinced. "A lawyer might tell Jimmy to get a blood test first, just to make sure."

"You'd want them to have DNA tests?"

"I don't know. It seems like there should be some way to make sure, though."

"That's fine. I want Mac to have the right father just as much as you do."

"That I doubt," he murmured. His gaze dropped to the child. He was kicking his bare feet as if he was trying to get somewhere. McLintocks walked by the time they were nine months old. His mother used to say she wondered why they were in such a hurry to get someplace they'd never seen.

"I think those kinds of tests can take weeks to get results," she cautioned.

"We'll figure it out."

"I'm sure you will." She leaned back in the chair and took a sip of the hot coffee. "I have to admit that I'm relieved. I think Jimmy is willing to take care of Mac, don't you?"

Jack didn't think that his brother had a clue about what it would take to be a father, but he didn't say so. It would be his job to educate Jimmy-Joe on his responsibilities, not Grace's. "Have you ever been married?"

"Uh, no."

"No?"

"No." She took another sip of her coffee and looked toward the outbuildings. "Aren't you usually working by now?"

"It's Sunday," he pointed out. "We try to take it easy."

"Oh."

It was easier making conversation with a six-month-old baby. Jack wiggled his fingers at the child, and the little boy moved his fist in the air. "I think he's trying to wave."

"He's too young," Grace said.

"But he's smart."

She started to smile. "You're saying that runs in the family?"

"Well, I—"

"Jack, you've got to see this," Jimmy-Joe said, bursting onto the porch. "Excuse me," he said, stepping in front of Grace and handing Jack a scrapbook. "See that review?"

Jack turned the book right side up and looked at a newspaper photograph of Jimmy dressed as a middle-aged man. "*The Odd Couple?*" he asked. "I remember that one."

"In San Antonio," Jimmy pointed out, tapping the page with his index finger. "A year ago last March. Every weekend for four weeks. I *knew* something didn't seem right when you said 'March.'"

"You could have met Lucy then," Grace suggested.

"Except I was dating a little gal who lived outside of San Antone. She, uh, kept me pretty busy. And gave me a place to live. I couldn't have been in Dallas, not even for one night." He turned to Jack. "Remember how I used to come home on Mondays and fall asleep when I should have been helping you guys with the calving?"

"I remember." And he did, now that Jimmy described it.

Jimmy sprawled in his chair and looked at Mac. "Sorry, kid, but I guess I'm just your uncle." He looked at Jack. "We could keep him, anyway, you know. You and Isabella could—"

"That's what Jet thought, too. Does it ever occur to anyone around here that Bella and I have raised enough kids? She's going to retire, and I might, too."

"You can't retire," Jimmy scoffed. "You're only thirty-six."

"I can do any damn thing I please," he pointed out. "In one week and five days." Which wasn't exactly the truth, but he figured he had a right to his privacy.

"Excuse me," Grace said in that soft voice that made him want to take her to bed. "Could we talk about Mac, please? Could someone explain what we should do next?"

"*We* do next?" Jack asked.

She wasn't intimidated. "Where were you a year ago last March, Mr. McLintock?"

He figured she'd called him 'Mr. McLintock' to annoy him, so he plastered a smile on his face to show her he wasn't bothered at all. "Calving, I would imagine."

Jimmy hopped to his feet. "Want me to check the book?"

"What book?" Grace asked.

"No," Jack said. "I will."

"What book?" Grace asked once again.

Aw, hell. He didn't want to explain the book to a city girl. "I keep a record of all ranch business. That way we can tell what we sold, when we bred the cows, when we bought the new tractor, things like that."

Jimmy nodded, a smile on his face. "And it would tell what Jack was doing that March, too, I'll bet."

"I don't write down everything," he felt obligated to point out. "I sure as hell don't put personal stuff down."

"You don't *have* any personal stuff," Jimmy said. "You wouldn't have anything to write down."

"Thanks for pointing that out."

"Hey, no problem." Jimmy flashed Grace a movie-star smile. "He's grumpy in the morning. Have you noticed?"

"I'm catching on," she said. She pulled the stroller out of the way as Jack headed for the door and went inside. "This is turning out to be a busy morning."

Jimmy yawned and stretched. "Here I thought I was coming home to go to bed, and in about twenty minutes I find out I'm a father and then I'm not a father and then maybe I'm an uncle." He closed his eyes and yawned again. "Wake me up when you find out what my official title is going to be, okay?"

"It might take a while."

"That's okay," he mumbled. "I could use the rest."

With that he appeared to go to sleep. Grace smiled as Jimmy started to snore. He seemed like a nice young man; he'd been willing to take Mac to Hollywood with him. He'd suggested, as Jet had, that they keep Mac, anyway. It was easy for them to assume that their older brother wouldn't mind taking care of one more person, but Grace had seen the expression on Jack's face. He was a man who wasn't interested in fatherhood. So Grace sipped her coffee, listened to the birds, made smiley faces at the baby and waited for Jack to return with the mysterious book.

"YOU WERE IN DALLAS," Jethro pointed out, following Jack onto the porch. "That has to mean something."

"Shh," Grace whispered. "Jimmy's asleep."

"It means I was in Dallas, that's all. It doesn't mean I went to bed with a stranger and fathered a child." Jack sat down, took a sip of cold coffee and tossed the rest into a sad-looking flower bed. He glanced toward Jimmy. "That boy could sleep through a dynamite blast."

Jet tipped his hat to Grace. "Good morning, Grace. Mornin', Mac," he said to the child, then sat down in the remaining chair. He tilted his hat back and looked around him. "This is a pretty sorry place for a family meeting. Now, if the courtyard was cleaned up, we could have ourselves some better scenery."

"Feel free to go back there and dig, weed and plant during your spare time," Jack told him. "No one would mind."

"Isabella would have my hide."

"Why?" Grace couldn't help asking.

"She thinks we'll put all the flowers in the wrong

places," Jet said. "And she figures she's going to get it all done by herself in the next two weeks."

"It will be beautiful for the party," Grace said. "Isabella told me you were going to have it there."

"Yep. If it gets done in time."

"It'll get done," Jack declared. "Everything will get done."

"The band's coming early to help."

Grace wanted to laugh at Jack's expression. He didn't look at all impressed with that news.

"Why?"

"To help out."

"They get kicked out of another apartment?"

"Well..."

Mac let out a loud wail, Jimmy stopped snoring, and the other two men looked at Grace for help. She unhooked him from the seat belt and lifted him into her arms.

"What's the matter with him?"

"That meant he was tired of sitting by himself when there were lots of people with laps."

Jack nodded. "Smart kid."

Jet agreed. "Yep. But what are we going to do about him?" He looked at his older brother. "You're sure you didn't have a little too much fun in Dallas at the equipment show?"

"I'm sure," he said through gritted teeth. "I looked at tractors. I had a couple of drinks with some of the boys from Santa Fe. I went to bed. Alone."

"So, if it's not you, not me and not Jimmy, then—"

"We're not a hundred percent sure about you."

Jet nodded. "I'll take care of that. Then what?"

"We're going to talk to Jason."

Jimmy opened his eyes and struggled to sit up. "Jason? Where is he?"

"We don't know. He called a few days ago and said he had things to do and wouldn't be home right away."

"What kind of things?"

Jack shrugged. "I didn't talk to him. Bella did."

Grace bounced Mac to make him giggle. "I can't stay here much longer." She looked at Jack; after all, he sat in the chair closest to her. "Should I take Mac with me?"

He didn't hesitate, just looked at her with those dark eyes. "We'll wait for Jason. Can you do that?"

"How long?"

"I don't know. Soon, I would think. Today, tomorrow, maybe."

Grace looked around her. Jet winked, Jimmy smiled, and a horse whinnied from somewhere over by the barn. There was an entire courtyard to weed and teenaged baby-sitters to hire. There was Jack, who had kissed her last night as if he found her irresistible. "All right. I'll stay until you talk to Jason, but if he's a McLintock you have to make plans for him."

Jack didn't smile. "Agreed" was all he said.

Mac chuckled and pulled her hair.

"WHAT THE HELL is she doing?"

"Weeding."

"I can see that," Jack said, standing with his hands

on his hips. He and Jet watched Grace from the glass
doors of the living room. The wall of doors was de-
signed to open onto the courtyard, but that part of the
house had been neglected since Jess McLintock died.
"But why?"

"I guess she felt like it" was all Jet could come up
with. He didn't have any idea why their houseguest
wanted to pull weeds, but if she did, why would Jack
want to stop her? He was always trying to get people to
work.

"She's not even wearing a hat. She could get heat
stroke."

"Well, get the woman a hat." Jet tried not to smile at
the expression on Jack's face. He looked like a man
who couldn't have what he wanted, a rare thing for
their oldest brother. Jet couldn't wait to tell Isabella
that he'd caught Jack pacing in the living room.

"We don't need a sick woman around here," Jack
grumbled. Jet turned back to watch Grace dig weeds
from between flat stones. She wore an old pair of
gloves and was on her knees digging with a small
spade. Mac sat in his stroller in the shade of the porch.
He was most likely sleeping, since his head was tilted
to the side. "Especially not now."

"Less than two weeks to go." Jet clapped his brother
on the back. "I'm going to Nashville, Jimmy's heading
for Hollywood, and Jason is going to grad school.
What are you going to do with your money, Jack? Buy
some more cows?"

Jack didn't answer for a few moments. "I don't

know," he said. "I haven't decided what I'll do. I'll give Isabella enough so she can retire."

"We'll all chip in for that," Jet agreed.

"And then, we'll see. I can't shake the feeling that something is missing. I don't have the talents the rest of you have. All I know is ranching, and yet sometimes I want to get into my car and drive away. Far away."

Jet didn't know what to say. He'd always pictured Jack as the solid older brother, the brother who would always be on the ranch, always available to solve any and all of his younger brothers' problems. "Maybe you spend too much time alone. You should get out more."

"Like I did Friday night?" He pointed to underneath his eye where the skin was still bruised and swollen. "I don't think so."

"Hey, you got to dance with a pretty woman. And you got to hear one of the new songs."

"I heard half of it," he said. "Until Greg Enders decided to fight."

"I'll play the rest at the party," Jet promised. "We don't have a gig next weekend so we have lots of time to practice. We decided not to take any more gigs until we hit Nashville. And we're all yours until the party."

Jack didn't seem to be impressed with that information. "Have you told Isabella that?"

"Oh, they're bringing their own food. And their own beer. Gus has an old trailer he's pulling behind his truck, so the guys won't be any trouble."

"I'll believe it when I see it," Jack said, still watching Grace. She'd made quite a pile of weeds.

"Maybe you should help her," Jet pointed out. Jack

needed a woman. Anyone could see that. "You could bring her a hat. And you could push the wheelbarrow."

He could tell Jack was thinking it over by the way he was scowling. Jack never looked happy when he was thinking. "I thought I'd take the truck and go out and check on the cows up north this afternoon. Unless you want to do it."

"I'll do it," Jack said. "Only I'm going on horseback. Last time I was up there the road was washed out."

"Why don't you take Grace up there with you? Show her another part of the ranch, keep her from working herself to death out in the courtyard."

"What about the baby?"

"I'll watch him."

Jack turned and looked at him. "You? You don't know anything about babies."

"Hey, I'm going to make a pretty damn good uncle."

"You sure you want to have that test tomorrow?"

Jet shrugged. "I need to know if I'm shooting blanks or not. But I'm damn sure I haven't had sex without using a rubber, so there's no chance of my being Mac's father."

"I've got to find out who is." They both looked over to the sleeping child. "If he's not one of ours there's no sense worrying about it."

"And if he is?"

"We'll do what we can," Jack promised. "Whatever that is."

Jet chuckled. "I think Grace is going to make sure of that."

"She's a pain in the neck."

"You like her."

Jack shrugged. "I don't have a lot of experience with women."

"At least you recognize a pretty one when you see one." Jet nudged his brother toward the door. "Go see if she wants to go riding with a cowboy. Quit worrying about the kid and concentrate on being with a woman."

Jet strolled out of the living room to the kitchen. It was Bella's day off, but he'd find her. He couldn't wait to tell her that he was right, after all: Jack had his mind on something else besides cattle.

"YOU DON'T HAVE TO DO that," a low voice said. Grace had seen Jack's shadow before he spoke, but she didn't stop pulling weeds. She liked to pull weeds. She liked plants, although she was used to plants in pots. She'd have to call her neighbor and ask if she would water her plants.

"I don't mind," she said without looking up. She could see the toes of his dusty brown boots near the pile of weeds. "I can't just sit around doing nothing."

"You don't have to work," he insisted.

"I don't mind. This is a beautiful courtyard. Isabella said you're having the party out here."

"Part of it," he said, stepping in front of her. He sat on his haunches so she had no choice but to look at him. He was better-looking than his younger brothers. More solid, with less charm and more substance. She liked the younger boys, but they still seemed like young men. Jack McLintock was very much a grown man.

Don't fall in love with a cowboy. There was little chance of that, Grace decided. This particular cowboy didn't spend much time talking or smiling. She waited for Jack to say something else, and when he didn't she looked down at the skinny row of weeds between the flat stones.

"If you're going to be outside you should be wearing a hat," he said, holding out a worn brown Stetson. She took it and put it on. And felt like Annie Oakley.

"Thanks."

"Now you're ready." He stood and held out his hand. "Come on."

It was ridiculously easy to put her hand in his and let him help her to her feet. It was ridiculously hard to pull her hand away from those rough, warm fingers. She brushed the dirt from her jeans. "Ready for what?"

"You said you've never been on a horse." He waved toward the direction of the barn. "I have a couple saddled and ready to go."

"But Mac—"

"Will be with Isabella. She and her granddaughters are arguing right now over who is going to get him first."

"They are?" She looked over to the baby, who still slept peacefully in his stroller. "He's going to wake up soon."

"They're prepared. And eager."

"And very nice," Grace added. "They've been a big help."

"That's what families are for," Jack said. "And Isabella and her family have been on this ranch longer than I have."

"You're very lucky."

"Yeah," he said, adjusting the brim of his hat. She couldn't see the expression in his eyes now. "Now and then."

"Is it a very tame horse?"

She thought she saw him smile. "And old, too. We'll take it slow."

Grace somehow doubted that.

6

"PUT YOUR LEFT FOOT in the stirrup and swing yourself up."

Easy for him to say. Grace eyed the animal, who suddenly appeared to be three stories high. The horse shook his head and stomped one foot. "What does that mean?" She pictured the horse thinking, *No way am I going to let that woman from Dallas climb on top of me.*

"Flies."

"Oh." The horse looked forward again and stood patiently while Jack held his reins in one hand. Grace grabbed the saddle horn, stuck her booted foot in the stirrup and managed to sprawl against the animal's side.

"Throw your right leg over and you're all set."

She did and she was. Barely. And she hadn't looked graceful, either. "I wish you'd given me a shorter horse."

"Cobble may be a little on the tall side, but he's as tame as they come. And almost twenty years old."

"That's good?"

"That's old." He handed her the reins. "Hold these in one hand, like this. You are right-handed, aren't you?"

"Yes."

"Okay, then hold the reins in your right hand. When you want to go left, press the reins against the right side of his neck. When you want to go right, press the reins against the left side of his neck. When you want him to move, nudge his sides with your heels. Those boots okay?"

She'd borrowed them from Lina. "Fine. And what do I do when I want to stop?"

"Pull back. Gently. If you do it too hard, he'll stop short and you'll fly over his head."

Grace gulped. "Well, I wouldn't want to do that."

"No. Not your first time in the saddle, anyway." Jack swung easily onto a heavily muscled palomino and gathered the reins. He looked exactly like every cowboy in every western movie she'd ever seen.

"Hi, Cobble," Grace said, patting the horse nervously on the neck. He was a nondescript brown color; his mane and tail were sparse and a shade darker than the rest of him. "Is he named for apple cobbler?"

Jack looked over his shoulder and gave her a strange look. "No. He came to us as Cobble. I don't know why." He brought his horse around to stand beside hers. "We'll walk for a while, until you get used to being in the saddle."

"A while" had better be about six hours. Her horse started up on his own as soon as Jack nudged his into a walk, so Grace hung on to the saddle horn with one hand and the reins with the other. She refused to topple from the saddle. If she broke any bones she wouldn't be able to take care of Mac. She didn't want to think about how much she'd miss him when she left.

Instead, she looked at Jack's broad back. His horse kept pulling ahead, and Jack kept bringing him back to fall into place beside Grace and Cobble.

"Sorry," he said, reining the prancing horse. "He likes to be first, and he likes to go fast."

"You won't go fast, will you?"

"No." He smiled, which made him look much younger. "I'll stay here with you."

Grace didn't know why the simple sentence gave her a lump in her throat. Maybe because no one had promised such a simple thing before.

"What's wrong?" He drew closer. "If you're that scared, we don't have to ride. I thought you'd enjoy—"

"I'm fine," she managed to say. "I was just thinking about something else, that's all."

"Keep your mind on your riding," he said. "Or you'll wind up sitting in the dust."

Grace laughed. "Okay, cowboy. I'll pay attention."

"See that you do." He smiled again, only this time Grace's heart pounded just a little bit faster. Which, she told herself, was silly. She was twenty-nine years old, and much too mature to react this way to a set of wide shoulders and a Stetson.

They rode in the opposite direction from where they'd been yesterday. This time he guided her north, over some gentle hills and along a trail lined with the occasional mesquite. A hot breeze blew against her back and sent tendrils of hair against her cheeks. The old hat shaded her from the relentless sun, and the long-sleeved shirt she'd borrowed from Isabella protected her skin. She began to relax, especially since

Cobble showed no signs of wanting to race the restless palomino. She loosened her grip on the saddle horn. Jack pointed out various cattle and their little calves, explained how the ranch was run and described how hard he and his brothers had worked to keep the place going over the years. He seemed to want her to understand what a hard life ranching was.

So she listened. And she thought of Mac growing up on this Texas ranch. He would work hard, but he would have a father and uncles and the grandmotherly Isabella to love him. He would be where he belonged, and he would grow up knowing it. No matter how difficult this weekend had been, Grace knew that she was doing the right thing.

They rode for more than an hour, until Jack halted before a shaded spot by a shallow pond.

"You ready for a break?"

"Yes." Her thighs were protesting the hour on the saddle, but she didn't want to complain. Cobble had behaved himself nicely. She attempted to pull back on the reins, but the horse stopped voluntarily before she said, "Whoa. Will he hold still while I get off?"

Jack swung out of the saddle and walked over to her. "He's not going anywhere," he assured her. "Just get off the opposite way you got on."

"That's easy for you to say." Her muscles refused to cooperate. "You'll have to give me a minute."

"Here," he said, lifting up his arms. Grace let him help her from the horse and stand her on her feet in the grass. He didn't release her until she told him she was fine. It took only a few minutes for her feet to work, and Jack returned to his horse and unpacked his saddlebag.

Grace took off her hat and ran her fingers through her hair. She stayed in the shade, then sat down with her back against a tree trunk when Jack came over with a canteen.

"Have some water," he said, handing it to her. He unwrapped a package of sandwiches and cookies and put it between them. "I brought lunch," he declared. "It isn't much, but it was the best I could do on short notice. I'll bet you were too busy to eat breakfast."

"This is great," she told him, surprised at how hungry she was. She'd made herself some toast after she'd fed Mac, but she hadn't thought about lunch for herself. She helped herself to what looked like a roast beef sandwich. "I'm impressed that you thought of it. Thank you."

"No problem." He sat down and took a sandwich for himself. "We always carry water when we head out."

"Why are you doing this?"

"Doing what?"

"Taking me out here. Showing me more of your ranch. Fixing lunch."

He didn't answer right away. "I guess I wanted you to know what kind of life Mac is going to have here."

"That's what I thought." She took a bite of her sandwich. Okay, she was right. It was because of Mac and not because he liked her. It was a ridiculous thought, anyway. "I think he'll have a good life here with one of you. Were you hoping I'd take him back to Dallas?"

"I don't know." He ate half of his sandwich before speaking again. "I guess I was hoping to get to know you better. It's not easy to try to figure all this out. I've never been faced with anything like this before."

"What do you want to know?"

He studied her with that familiar serious expression. "Why did you get involved in this?"

"I told you. I made a promise."

"But why? Surely it was up to the state authorities to find the child's real father."

"And put him in a foster home until they figured it out—if ever? No." She said it more emphatically than she would have wished, because his dark eyebrows rose.

"You have something against foster homes?"

She lifted her chin. "I've lived in a few. Some were wonderful and some weren't."

"Where were your parents?"

"No one knew." It wasn't hard to say it anymore. Not really. If she kept her tone very matter-of-fact, then Jack wouldn't think it bothered her. "No one ever found out."

"How old were you?"

"Four. I never knew who my father was. I don't even know if my mother knew. One day she left me at day-care and never came back to get me. No one ever found her or discovered what happened."

"People don't just disappear," he said, clearly bewildered.

"Of course they do." She set the remaining section of

her sandwich on the aluminum foil and took a sip of water from the canteen. "It happens all the time."

"Were you eventually adopted?"

"No." She slapped a fly that landed on her leg. "By the time anyone got around to figuring out that my mother wasn't going to come back, I was too old for anyone to want to adopt me."

There was a long moment of silence. "And that's why Mac is going to have his own home."

"That's right." She looked toward the horses, who grazed on the sparse grass under the trees. "When you and your brothers get around to figuring out what to do with him, I'll go back to Dallas knowing I did the right thing."

"I see." And he looked as if he did. He climbed to his feet and held out his hand to help her up. "I just hope it works out the way you think it should."

"It will," she promised, putting her hand in his. He helped her stand, but he didn't release her. They were very close to each other and neither moved.

"You're very sure of yourself," he whispered, his head dipping toward hers.

"I have to be." He had a beautiful mouth, she thought as his lips touched hers. She should have expected to feel that tug of longing, that irresistible pull toward him. Grace moved into his embrace and felt those solid arms wrap around her. Her breasts were against his chest, her hands on his shoulders, her mouth on his. It wasn't the tentative kiss of last night. He urged her lips apart; she wanted him closer. He explored her mouth; she gripped his shoulders to keep from falling as her body turned soft and hot.

He slowly withdrew and gently set her away from him. She didn't know what to do with her arms, so she smoothed her palms on her jeans and looked around for her hat. Jack picked it up from the grass and handed it to her.

"We'd better get back." He stood there and didn't move.

"Yes," she managed to say, but her heart pounded loud enough to scare the horses.

"I guess you've seen enough."

And felt enough. Her gaze went to his lips, then higher, to those dark eyes that gave her no clue as to what he was thinking. "Yes."

He brought the horses over and helped her mount Cobble. He paused, his hand touching her leg. "I'm not going to apologize," he said.

"Good." She adjusted her hat and attempted to hide how much he affected her. "I've never been kissed by a cowboy before. Not until this weekend, that is."

He smiled, just a little. "I don't dare ask you how cowboys compare to the men in Dallas."

"There were no men in Dallas," she told him. She wanted him to know she didn't go around falling into the arms of any man who kissed her.

Jack shook his head, climbed onto his horse and picked up the reins. "Sweetheart, I can't believe they're not falling at your feet."

"Now you're teasing."

He winked at her and swung his horse toward

home, leaving Cobble and Grace to follow. Grace smiled. She liked it when he didn't look as if he had the weight of Texas on his shoulders. She eyed those shoulders and remembered how strong he'd felt under her fingers. No wonder women loved cowboys. They *felt* so darn good.

NAKED WOMEN DECORATED the side of the old school bus. Black curtains covered the windows, and blue smoke poured from the exhaust pipe as the bus bounced into the yard. Jet stood in the yard and directed the bus driver to an empty area where the chicken house used to be before it burned down, and Jack reined in his horse and watched the monstrosity find a home next to the best outhouse on the property.

Cobble brought Grace up next to him. "What is it?"

"Can't you guess?"

"How?"

"From the painting." He sighed. "That's the tour bus for Jet and the Naked Ladies."

"You're kidding."

"No. They've come for the party, Jet said, but they've actually been kicked out of another apartment."

"They're going to stay here?"

"I'm afraid so. Probably until they leave for Nashville."

"In two weeks."

"Yes."

"Why is everyone leaving in two weeks?"

Jet waved and called to them, so Jack was saved

from having to explain. Their grandfather's strange trust fund was pretty much public knowledge, and the folks around town were ready to help the McLintocks celebrate, but Jack hesitated to explain it to Grace. He didn't think she was here for the money anymore, but he couldn't take the chance. And he didn't have time to discuss his crazy family, not when his brother's crazy band was spilling out of the bus.

One of them went inside the outhouse, but the other four gathered around Jet and began to walk in their direction.

"I don't think I've ever seen anything like that," Grace said, still looking at the side of the bus. "It's obvious the ladies are naked, but the guitars hide everything so well."

"Yeah," Jack said, climbing off his horse. "It's real art, all right." He came over to her side. "You need some help getting down?"

"Sure."

He touched her for the first time since they'd headed for home. Since he'd put her out of his arms instead of making love to her. This time Grace managed to dismount with less awkwardness, but Jack still had the pleasure and pain of taking her by the waist and holding her steady as she touched the ground. She was small and delicate under his palms. Beads of sweat broke out on his forehead, and Jack took his hands away from that tempting little body. He had no business kissing a woman from Dallas, or kissing anyone, for that matter.

"There," he said, backing away from her. "I hope you're not sore tomorrow."

"I'll be fine." She flexed her knees a couple of times and continued to hold Cobble's reins. "Do we take the horses to the barn now?"

"To the corral," he said, "but I'll take care of—" Jet and his friends approached them, and the drummer hurried out of the outhouse and caught up with the others.

"Hey, Jack!" Jet grinned at both of them. "First you'd better say hi to the guys in the band. They want to thank you for letting them crash here."

Jack shook hands with the men while Jet introduced Grace as a "friend of the family." She told them she liked their bus and Jack winced. Isabella was going to pitch a fit over that chunk of rusty metal being parked within sight of her grandchildren.

"We're going to set up in the slaughterhouse and start practicing," Jet said.

"No one's been in there in years. You sure you want to put expensive equipment out there?"

"I've been cleaning it up," he replied, taking Jack aside.

Grace was asking the men about Nashville, and they were practically tripping over themselves to answer her. The horses stood there patiently, which was more than Jack could say for himself.

"I've got it looking pretty good," Jet was saying, "but we're going to need some more extension cords."

"In the east shed, on the wall over by the window."

"Thanks." Jet glanced over at Grace. "How was your ride?"

"Fine."

"She looked at you and blushed. That's a good sign."

"Like hell."

"Seriously," Jet insisted. "I saw her when you helped her from her horse. Which wasn't exactly necessary. She looked capable of climbing down from old Cobble without you holding on to her."

"I didn't mind."

Jet chuckled. "No, I'm sure you didn't mind at all."

Jack looked over his brother's shoulder as a truck and trailer pulled into the yard. "Looks like Gus has arrived."

"Great! He's got the food." Jet hurried over to talk to him, and Jack returned to the group of men gathered around Grace. He'd known most of them since they were teenagers. They were a decent group, just a little rowdy. And they loved to play music. Jack took the reins from Grace as the men hurried over to greet the bass player.

"I'll take care of the horses," he said.

"Thanks." She smiled at him again, and his heart did strange things in his chest. "I'd better go check on Mac." She hesitated before walking away. "Thanks for teaching me how to ride."

He tipped his hat. "Any time."

Jack watched her walk toward the house before he turned away and led the horses to the corral. Their ride hadn't exactly been much of a workout, but he felt like he'd been put through the wringer. He couldn't believe she'd only been here three days and already he was worn out.

"YOU DON'T THINK he's too little?"

Isabella folded her arms across her chest and studied the baby as he sat in the high chair. "I think he likes it."

"Really?"

"Look at him." Isabella smiled with grandmotherly pride. "He likes being a big boy and sitting there."

Mac grinned as if he understood what she said and slapped his little hand on the plastic tray. When he realized it made a noise, he did it again. Several times.

"I guess you're right," Grace said, keeping a careful eye on the child. "He can't fall out?"

"No. There are safety straps, and I put a little pillow around him to prop him up." She clapped her hands and made the baby chuckle. "Oh, what a big boy you are!"

Mac proudly banged the tray again, as if to show her just what a big boy he was.

"He's a McLintock, isn't he?" Grace asked.

"I think so," the older woman agreed. "He looks like the boys did when they were little."

"But none of the men are claiming him."

Isabella motioned for Grace to sit down. "They will have to," she said, pouring two glasses of lemonade. She brought them to the table and sat down opposite Grace. Mac practiced slapping the tray.

"Thank you."

"You and Jack had a nice ride?"

Grace smiled. "It was more like a 'walk,' but I got to see more of the ranch. It's a big place, isn't it?"

"Yes. And it means a lot to Jack. He's worked hard to keep it. You are going to stay?"

"For a little bit longer. Until Jason arrives."

"Jason isn't Mac's father," Isabella declared, her brown face creased with worry.

"Then, one of the others isn't telling the truth."

Isabella shrugged. "Jet is not the one. And Jimmy-Joe told me that he was in a play that month. He didn't even have a car that winter, and he already had a girlfriend."

"Having a girlfriend doesn't necessarily mean that he didn't, um, meet another woman."

"No, but Jimmy is loyal when he is in love. And he thought he was in love, until the girl left him for someone else."

"Why are you sure it's not Jet?" Mac squeaked, and Grace patted his soft little hands. He patted hers back.

"That is for him to say, but I think the chance is only very slight."

"Which leaves Jack." Grace could picture Lucy with Jack, but she didn't like thinking about it. Any woman would find him attractive and sexy and appealing, and Lucy had liked cowboys. She'd said they knew what they were doing and they took their sweet time doing it.

"I don't believe that, either," Isabella said, "but there's no denying the boy's chin. He had to get it from somewhere." She studied the child's face again. "But none of those boys would lie. That is what puzzles me."

Jason, Grace decided. He was the youngest and would have been intrigued with an older, experienced woman. She couldn't blame him. Lucy had been a woman who lived life to the fullest and enjoyed her men the same way. Now she was gone and here was Mac, a little boy who needed his daddy. "I should go back to Dallas," she said. "Maybe I should take him with me until all of this is straightened out."

"With Jet in Nashville and Jimmy in Hollywood? No." Isabella shook her head. "There is not enough time. They will all be gone soon, and whatever is decided has to happen in—"

"I know. Two weeks."

Isabella nodded and drank the last of her lemonade. "I don't have much time to get the courtyard ready. I heard you like to weed?"

Grace smiled. "I hope you don't mind."

"Mind? Of course not. Come," she said, standing up. "I'll show you what I have planned. You can help, I think."

"I'd like that. If you don't think I'd be in the way."

"In the way?" Isabella scoffed. "You're practically one of the family now."

Grace watched the woman extricate Mac from his high chair. *One of the family.* She liked the sound of that. At least for now.

"IT'S JASON," JET SAID, holding out the telephone receiver. Everyone at the long table stopped talking. Isabella had cooked up an extra pot of chili and had made sure all of the band members joined them for supper. Jack stood up and tossed his napkin on the table.

"I'll take it in the office."

"He wants to talk to Jimmy first." Jet spoke into the phone again. "Yeah, kid, we're eating chili. Isabella outdid herself again." He paused. "Yep, we're all set. Don't forget to bring it."

"Bring what?" Jack asked, moving around the table.

"His diploma," Jet said, then listened into the receiver again. "Yeah, okay. Sure."

Jimmy scraped his chair back and took the phone from Jet. "Hey, kid, how are you? Still smarter than the rest of us?"

Jack held up five fingers so that Jimmy would know that he was getting five minutes to chat with Jason and no more. He left the kitchen and hurried down the hall to his office to pick up the extension. He gave Jimmy a few minutes, then picked up the phone.

"Anytime," Jimmy was saying.

"Jason?" Jack wanted to hear the kid's voice. "Where are you?"

"Hi, Jack. I'm on my way home, don't worry."

"I *am* worried," he said, but hearing Jason's voice made him smile to himself. The kid sounded just fine. "We figured you got lost."

"Nah. I just had some stuff to do before I got home, that's all."

"What kind of 'stuff'?"

Jimmy broke into the conversation. "Hey, kid, I'm

going back to eat my dinner before anyone else gets it. See you later."

"Yeah, later," Jason said.

Jack heard a click, and then the connection became louder. "So, why aren't you here yet? We can't start the party without you."

"I've been packing, getting things together, you know. I've got a lot of things to talk to you about."

"Yeah? Well, get your butt home, then."

Jason laughed. "I'll be there. Tell me again when we meet with the lawyers."

"A week from Friday. At 9:00 a.m."

"I'll be there."

"You'd better be home before that, Jase. We could use you around here." He could hear Jason laugh.

"You can't wait to put me back on a horse and make me fix fences," he said. "How is everybody there? Everything okay?"

"It's fine," Jack fibbed. "Jet's band is here getting ready for the party. When are you coming? It better be soon."

"I'm bringing a surprise, too." Jason's voice grew serious. "Jack, I've got a lot of news."

"About going to England?"

"More than that. I'll tell you when I see you."

"Tell me now." He wasn't too thrilled with surprises, especially after the last few days.

"Nope. Can't. You have to see for yourself."

"I don't want—"

"I'll be home in a few days."

"When, exactly?"

"As soon as I can," Jason promised. "Tell everyone I said hi and tell Isabella that I can't wait to have chili again. Do you think she'll make my favorite?"

"She will, once she knows you're heading home."

"I'm on my way. Just give me a few more days."

"Okay, buddy," Jack said. "Take care, and don't be too long."

"See ya, Jack."

"Okay, kid. Take good care of yourself and come home safe."

He heard the receiver click, and then the dial tone. Then he realized Jason hadn't said where he was. He was bringing a surprise. He was on his way home.

Jack shoved his hands in his pockets and looked out the window. He knew he should rejoin the group seated around the kitchen table, but he really didn't feel like talking right now. He wanted that boy home. He needed to know if there was any chance that Jason was Mac's father. Because if he wasn't, there was only one other possibility.

And that didn't bear thinking about.

7

ON MONDAY MORNING Grace worked out a plan for the courtyard, one that involved flowers in big pots. Of course, the weeding had to be finished first. Isabella said that Jack planned to drape strands of little white lights along the porch eaves, and there would be tables filled with food lining the side that opened onto the kitchen.

"You must stay for the party," Isabella said, pushing the empty wheelbarrow beside her. "It is going to be so beautiful."

"I'm not very good at parties," Grace admitted, though she wanted to stay. She also knew she should leave, but she couldn't use work as an excuse. Work could wait; seeing that Mac was settled and cared for couldn't.

"Then, it's a good thing for me that you are good at planting flowers."

"Flowers are easy," she said, attacking another set of weeds. She looked over at Mac, who lay on a blanket in the shade where Marta and Mica watched over him. "Easier than children."

"You don't want to have children?"

"Oh, it's not that. I would love to have a family, but I worry that I don't know how to take care of Mac. I worry all the time that I'm doing something wrong."

"You are not," Isabella insisted. "He is a happy child, and a healthy one. The size of those thighs! My goodness!"

"He's going to be a big boy."

"And he will be fine," Isabella assured her. "You have nothing to worry about, except what you will wear to the party."

Grace shook her head and sat back on her heels. "I'll be long gone before then, so I'm not worrying about it." But she was running out of clothes, even though she'd washed the few things she brought with her. A sundress, a pair of shorts, jeans, some underwear and two shirts weren't getting her very far. "I wish Jason would show up soon."

"Jack told him to get home as soon as possible, but I don't think that boy was paying attention."

Grace thought he sounded irresponsible, but she didn't say so. Clearly Jason was a favorite of Bella's. The woman's face lit up whenever she talked about him.

"Well, it would sure help to talk to him."

"He has a scholarship to go to school in England. Did Jack tell you?"

"Yes. He said Jason was smart."

"And he writes poetry, too," the woman added, attacking weeds a few feet away. "His poems have won prizes at college."

"Maybe that's his surprise. A book of poetry."

Isabella's brown eyes lit up as she looked at Grace. "Oh, do you think so?"

"If he's a poet..."

"Of course. He's bringing us his first book. I never thought of that. I wonder if Jack thought of it."

"Thought of what?" a voice asked.

They turned around to see Jack tickle Mac's tummy. Grace answered, "We've been talking about Jason's surprise and what it might be. I thought of a book of poetry."

"Could be, I guess." He stood up. "I'm going to town. Do you need anything?"

"Take Grace," Isabella said. "She needs some clothes if she's going to stay here and wait for Jason."

"I don't—"

"Sure you do," the older woman said. "And this is your big chance to see Locklin. You don't want to miss out on that, do you?"

"I'm not ready to go to town."

"I'll wait for you to clean up." He looked at his watch. "If you hurry. I have a meeting at eleven-thirty."

Isabella shooed her away. "Go," she urged. "The girls and I will spoil your boy while you're gone. And you can pick up some groceries for me while you're in town."

Grace couldn't say no, not when Isabella needed groceries. She stood up and tried to brush the dirt from her jeans. "All right. I'll shower and put on my dress."

"I'll wait here," Jack said, and tickled Mac again.

Grace hurried as fast as she could. She grabbed her purse, made sure she had her credit card and check-book and was back in the courtyard twenty minutes later.

Jack looked at his watch, then at her. "Not bad" was all he said.

Grace thanked the girls, promised to bring them something special from town and kissed Mac's soft cheek. "Be a good boy," she told him, inhaling the sweet scent of baby powder. She'd bathed him this morning, the part of the day he loved the best. And she'd kissed his toes and tickled his feet and made silly noises on his belly so she could listen to him laugh.

"You're going to miss him," Jack said.

Grace didn't think it was very nice of him to point that out.

ARTIE BALLARD HELD UP one huge hand. "Stop right there, son," he drawled. "I am *not* hearin' this."

Jack glared back. "Then, how in hell am I supposed to tell you what's going on?"

"I'm your lawyer," Artie said, leaning forward in his huge leather chair. "But I can't tell you to break the law. It's against the rules." He leaned back, gave Jack a wink and said, "Let's speak hypothetically. About a rancher in Oklahoma. Let's call him John Wayne. Why don't you tell me a story about John Wayne?"

"I don't want to talk about anyone called John Wayne. I need some advice and I need it now. And I am *not* breaking any laws, by the way."

Artie sighed. "All right, boy. Go on."

"Like I said, she arrived with a baby and a birth certificate with the McLintock name on it."

"You have it?"

"Here's a copy." Jack took the folded paper from his

shirt pocket and handed it to Artie. The stocky lawyer, who looked more like a cattle auctioneer than one of the smartest lawyers north of San Antonio, unfolded the paper and examined it.

"What does she want?"

"She wants to give the baby to its father. Trouble is, none of us seems to be the father."

Artie chuckled. "That Jet oughta be more careful with his women. He's going to have to pay for this one."

Jack shook his head. "Jet had trouble with mumps when he was fifteen. I think he might be out of the fatherhood department. Jimmy-Joe was doing a play in San Antonio during the month that the baby was, uh, conceived, and his truck was broken. He had a girlfriend, too, so I don't think he was making trips to Dallas."

He put the paper to the side of his desk. "May I keep this?"

"Sure. I made extra copies."

"This woman showed you the original?"

"Yep."

"So that leaves you and Jason. And I'm goin' to assume that neither one of you should be called 'Daddy'?"

"If I'd made love to a redhead in Dallas, I'd remember," Jack declared.

Artie sighed. "So would I, son."

"But I didn't."

"I did," the lawyer said. "Twice. Only it was in Fort

Worth, on the fourth of July. I always liked redheads, and this one was no exception."

"Her name wasn't Lucy Bagwell, was it?"

"No. And I'm thinking of something that happened twenty-one years ago."

"So, you'd understand that I'd remember something that happened a year ago last March."

"Yep. Now, Jet, on the other hand, might have so many women he doesn't remember them all, but you—" Artie shrugged, making Jack feel more like a monk than a rancher. He tried to get the conversation back on track.

"I haven't talked to Jason about this, but he's been in school in Oklahoma. I can't picture him going to Dallas and, uh, getting into trouble."

"Neither can I, but boys will be boys."

"Not Jason. He's more serious, more into his books and his poems."

Artie's eyebrows rose. "You're saying—"

"No, that's not what I'm saying. As far as I know, he likes girls just fine. But he would have been too young for this woman."

The lawyer shook his head. "I've seen it all, son. No rules about young or old, as long as they're consenting adults."

"Jason's not the baby's father."

"Then the birth certificate's a fraud. You want me to send someone to Dallas to check it out?"

Jack took a deep breath. "Not yet. First I want you to send someone to El Paso to find my father."

"Aw, hell," Artie swore. "You're tellin' me you think that old son of a bitch is still alive?"

"He's the only McLintock, other than me, who could have been in Dallas a year ago March. I haven't seen him in years, but if anyone was going to get someone pregnant and then leave her high and dry, it would be J.T. He took off and left my mother often enough."

Artie stood up and went over to the bar. "I know it's early, but I don't give a good goddamn about the time. You want one, don't you?"

"No, I'd better not." He didn't want whiskey on his breath when he met Grace at Nellie's. He'd offered to buy her lunch, and right now he couldn't remember why he'd thought that was a good idea.

"How about coffee, then?"

"No, thanks."

Artie returned with his drink and sat down at his desk. "I don't want to scare you, Jack, but if your grandfather's lawyers get wind of this, there could be hell to pay." He pushed a button on the intercom. "Sally, bring me the McLintock files. All of them, please." He took a sip of his drink and turned back to Jack. "Have you decided what you're going to do about the ranch?"

"I planned to use the trust fund money to pay off the loans."

"Conner's offer still stands, far as I know."

"Yeah, I know. But I don't want to sell."

Artie shook his head. "That place has been in your family for what—eighty, ninety years?" Jack nodded. "Seems a shame to let it go now." He paused as the secretary brought the papers he'd requested, then left the room and closed the door behind her. "Let's see," he muttered, flipping through the papers until he found what he wanted. "Give me a minute, Jack. I want to check something here."

"He's probably not alive," Jack muttered. "No one's seen or heard from him in fifteen years."

"Hold on," the lawyer said, studying the papers in front of him.

"Someone must have shot him by now." Jack walked over to the window and pulled back a section of the vertical blinds. Locklin was busy at noon, despite the heat. He looked down from the second-story window and wondered where Grace had disappeared to. He wished she'd walk by. He wouldn't mind looking at her, though he'd have been better off if she'd never come to Locklin.

"I thought he was in prison."

"He got out years ago," Jack said, turning away from the window and letting the blinds fall back into place. "Biggest mistake Texas ever made."

"His crime wasn't that bad," Artie reminded him.

"He wasn't your father."

The lawyer sighed. "Sit down, Jack. Why do you think this baby could belong to J.T.? He must be in his sixties by now."

"Fifty-six," Jack replied.

Artie tapped the papers piled in front of him. "I'll go through these line by line. I don't want you to worry until we have something to worry about, but you and I both know that your grandfather's instructions were pretty damn clear. I'll have a friend of mine, an investigator, do a little checking. Nothing official."

"Fair enough. And what do I do in the meantime?"

"You wait."

Jack figured he'd been waiting for sixteen years, and he was getting damn sick of it. "What about Grace Daniels and the baby?"

Artie reached for his whiskey and drained the contents of the glass. "You keep her away from lawyers, that's for damn sure. You don't let her out of your sight, and you sure as hell don't let her know that J. T. McLintock might still be catting around Texas. Can you do that?"

"I can try. She seems to like the ranch."

The lawyer winked at him. "See that you keep her happy, son. At least until Jason turns twenty-one and all you boys have cashed your checks."

Jack shook Artie's hand and left the building. He'd never been comfortable lying, but there was more at stake than just his future. The boys had waited a long time, and as long as there was no hard information about Mac's father, Jack would have to hope that Jason wasn't the shy poet everyone thought he was.

Until he found out what the hell was going on, he'd be nice. Even if it killed him.

"EVERYONE IS SO FRIENDLY," Grace told the salesclerk. She stepped closer to the mirror and turned to see if the shorts fit her properly.

"It's a nice town," the young woman agreed, then made a face. "Sometimes it's too small, if you know what I mean. Those shorts look good on you. Nice color."

"Thanks." So far she'd found another sundress, three T-shirts and these cotton shorts. She hadn't intended to buy so many clothes, but everything was on sale and there was lots to choose from. She returned to the dressing room and changed back into her sundress. Then she decided what she was going to buy and carried the items over to the register. "I guess I'm all set."

The young woman stopped folding T-shirts and started ringing up Grace's purchases. "Where are you from?"

"Dallas."

"And you're shopping in Locklin?"

Grace chuckled. "I didn't have much choice. I've ended up staying here longer than I planned."

"We don't get a lot of visitors out here," the young woman said, smiling. "But I'm glad you came. At least it will look like I did my job today."

"Do you know the McLintock family?"

"Everyone in town does." The girl looked at her with some awe. "Is that who you're visiting?"

"Yes."

"Are you some kind of relative?"

Grace hesitated. She couldn't remember what Jack had told her to say, so she opted for something close to the truth. "I'm a family friend."

"Wow. Lucky you, getting to stay with Jet McLintock. Have you heard him sing?"

"Yes, last Friday. I bet he'll be a big star someday."

"My momma won't let me go to the Stampede, so I

haven't heard his new songs." The salesclerk sighed and finished punching the numbers into the cash register. "Cash or charge?"

"Charge." Grace handed her a credit card.

"Thanks." She completed the sale, handed Grace the card and the receipt and started putting the clothes in a bright pink bag. "I guess you're here for the big party they're having. Sure is nice they're finally getting their money. Everyone in town thought Old Man Freemont was crazy for writing up his will the way he did."

"Really?" Grace tucked her wallet in her purse and hoped the girl would continue.

"Oh, yes. My grandfather said Mr. Freemont couldn't take his money with him when he died, so he wasn't going to let anyone else have it, either. 'Course, he hated old J.T. and the way he treated his daughter."

"He did?" She knew she shouldn't listen to gossip, but anything that concerned the McLintocks concerned Mac, and naturally anything that concerned Mac concerned her.

The girl handed her the bag and lowered her voice, even though there was no one else in the small store. "The second time Jet's father landed himself in prison was the last straw for old Mr. Freemont. My grandpa said that everyone in town was talking about the will for days, how Mr. Freemont didn't want his grandsons to turn out like their father and waste all his hardearned money."

The bell rang as another customer walked in, so Grace thanked the girl and left. She blinked against the harsh afternoon sun and reached in her purse for her sunglasses. Well, that had been interesting. She'd bought herself a summer wardrobe and learned that the McLintocks were going to inherit some money. No wonder Jack thought her arrival with Mac was suspicious. He must have thought she and Mac were after his money. Jack and his brothers could keep it, for all she cared. All that mattered was that one of them came forward to take care of Mac. Grace looked at her watch and then crossed the street. She had an hour to shop before meeting Jack for lunch, and she didn't want to waste any time.

HE TOOK HER TO NELLIE'S for hamburgers and chocolate shakes. He carried her packages, though he couldn't figure out how she could find so much to buy. He bought her an ice cream cone at the Dairy King outside of town. And when she congratulated him on inheriting his grandfather's money, Jack almost drove the car into a ditch.

"I think it's wonderful," Grace continued. "Now I understand why everyone is leaving and why you're having such a special party."

"Who told you?" was all he could manage to say.

"A salesclerk in the—" she rustled through her bags and read the name from the pink one "—Crystal Butterfly. Nice store, too. They were having a sale."

He should have known that people would talk. No one said much to his face, though George at the hardware store had clapped him on the back and said, "See you next Saturday."

"Jack?"

He glanced over at her. She wore that flowered dress that he liked, and her hair was loose and wavy. It looked soft, like her skin. Artie had said to keep her happy. She looked happy, even though she knew something about Grandpa's will. He wondered just how much. "What?"

"What's the matter? Was it a secret?"

"Nothing in Locklin's a secret, Grace. But I didn't think people were talking about it to strangers."

"She—the salesclerk—said everyone was really happy for you. It wasn't said in a mean way."

"Fine." He told himself it didn't matter, that as long as no one knew that J.T. might still be alive then everything would turn out fine.

"And she didn't think I was a stranger, since I said I was staying at the ranch. I told her I was a friend of the family."

So much for the "cousin" explanation. "You didn't mention Mac, did you?"

He saw her frown at him. "Of course not."

They rode in silence for a few miles until she spoke again. "Did you think that I came here for the money?"

"The thought did cross my mind."

"Mac doesn't need your money," Grace said, her voice low and quiet. "He just needs a home."

"If he belongs to one of us, he'll get what he needs," Jack said. He didn't know how he could promise anything more than that. Even to Grace.

"IS THIS SOME KIND of trick?"

"Just get into the truck," Jet hollered. Jimmy-Joe had

to have an explanation for everything. He opened the door and got in.

"Damn it, Jet," he grumbled. "What's your hurry?"

Jet put the truck into gear and stepped on the gas. A flock of chickens scattered out of the way and ran for their lives. "We have work to do."

"*Work?* Jack's gone to town and I just finished cleaning out the barn. Jack got me up at five-thirty."

"You had yesterday off," Jet pointed out, steering the truck toward the north pasture. "And I spent most of my day working with those horses Jack wants to sell." He'd also spent twenty minutes in a doctor's office, but he wasn't about to start talking about *that*. Talk about embarrassing, especially with Doc Reynolds's pretty nurse giving him a plastic cup and leading him toward the bathroom.

"Where are we going?"

"The road's washed out up here. I thought we'd dig it out and put some boards in so Jack can get the truck up to those pastures. It'll be faster that way."

"Faster for who?"

"Jack."

Jimmy yawned and pushed his hat back. "You want to tell me why Jack needs to do things fast?"

"Well, for one thing, he's going to be doing the work alone. Except for Lina and Ed. Isabella's talking about retiring and growing flowers, so there's going to be a lot of work for one man."

"I thought Jack was going to hire more help."

"He hasn't said anything lately." Jet guided the

truck over the hill and then gave it some more gas. "Maybe he's changed his mind."

"Jack doesn't change his mind."

That was true. "It's not important," Jet said. "Right now, I'm trying to give Jack time to find himself a woman. So he won't be lonely after all of us leave. He's never been alone."

Jimmy took some time thinking that over. "What about Grace? She seems nice enough, and she's pretty good-looking, too."

"Yep. Bella and I already talked it over. Jack seems to like her, and she even seems to like him. So all we have to do is give them time to be together."

"That's why we're fixing the road?"

"Yeah. And I'm gonna come up with some other ideas, too. Like takin' over Jack's chores." He looked over to his brother and grinned. "Pretty good thinkin', huh?"

"I don't know where you get your ideas," the younger man groaned.

"I get 'em all the time. That's why I've written so many songs and why the folks in Nashville are going to love me."

Jimmy leaned back and closed his eyes. "Hollywood's going to be a piece of cake compared to ranching in Texas."

"GIVE HIM TO ME," Jimmy said. "I'll tell him a story."

Jet reluctantly placed Mac in Jimmy's arms. "He'd rather hear me sing. You'll just put him to sleep again."

"He's a baby," Jimmy pointed out, settling Mac

against his wide chest. "He's supposed to go to sleep at night when people tell him stories." He looked across the living room to where Grace sat on the couch. "Right, Grace?"

"Well, I don't—"

"Stop it, you two," Jack drawled. He handed Grace a small plate that held a generous piece of chocolate cake. "Don't let them bother you, Grace." He smiled, and her heart melted a little bit more. "They may look grown up, but they're just big kids."

"Jet's just upset 'cause he's sitting home on a Friday night," Jimmy teased.

"They're not bothering me," she insisted. And, re-membering the plate in her hand, she added, "Thank you."

"Isabella's in a baking frenzy this week." With his own dessert in his hand, Jack sat down beside her. He looked over to his brothers. "You two can get your own, right, Bella?"

The old woman sat down in the rocking chair and patted her empty lap. "Give me the baby, Jimmy, and go get your cake."

He did as he was told, Jet following close behind. Mac snuggled against Bella's ample bosom and closed his eyes. "There, there," she crooned. "You dream sweet dreams, little man."

Oh, dear. What Lucy had warned her about was happening, and Grace looked around the living room and realized she should have left days ago. She should have gone home to her empty apartment and rejoiced in the solitude. She shouldn't be helping Isabella clean up the kitchen or be spending the dark evening hours relaxing with men who had worked hard all day and enjoyed something to eat before heading to bed. Soon, too soon, she would return to Dallas and curse the silence.

"Grace?" Jack's voice broke into her thoughts, and she turned to face him.

"What?"

"Is something wrong?"

"I was thinking about work," she said. "I can't remember the last time I've been away from the computer for so long." Jack had gone out of his way to be nice these past few days. She'd watched the way his brothers respected him, the way they helped one another with all of the ranch chores. The McLintock brothers were a close-knit family. And they were still waiting for Jason, waiting for the last piece of the puzzle to fall into place.

"What do you do?" Jack asked.

"I design software programs for small companies. Do you have a computer with a modem here?"

He shook his head. "I've got something I bought years ago. It works okay, I guess, but none of us ever got into it. What's a modem?"

"I guess you don't know what e-mail is, either," she said, trying not to laugh at the confused expression on that handsome face of his.

"Nope. And if it has to do with computers, I don't want to know."

"I could teach you," she offered, taking another bite of her cake.

Jet stretched out on the floor by her feet. "You might as well teach a skunk to sell perfume, Grace. Jack's not known for trying new things."

"That's not true," Jack said, winking at Grace. "Didn't I install indoor plumbing in the bunkhouse?"

"Yeah," Jet drawled. "And I wrote that song about it. Gets a laugh every time, too."

"Oh, Jet." Isabella chuckled. "You should stop with the silly songs. Your love songs are the best of all."

"That's what all the ladies say," Jet said. "Right, Jimmy?"

His younger brother shrugged. "I don't listen to what the ladies say about you. I'm too busy listening to what they're saying about *me*."

Jack set his empty plate on the table and picked up his glass of iced tea. "You two are going to be famous some day, I guess, but you'll never grow up."

Jimmy leaned in the doorway. "Do you have any brothers to boss you around, Grace?"

"No," she said lightly. "I always envied my friends who had older brothers, though."

Jack shook his head. "Wait until you meet Jason. He might have a few things to say about older brothers that you've never heard before."

"We've been good to the little guy," Jimmy said.

"Most of the time," Jet added, then they both began to laugh.

Isabella shushed them all. "You'll wake up the baby," she said. "And you two played too many tricks on Jason. I'm surprised he never got even with you."

Jack touched Grace's shoulder. "You don't have to

answer any questions," he told her, his voice low. "The boys don't mean any harm."

"Of course they don't," she said. "I think they're great."

"Yeah," he agreed. "They're pretty good guys."

"You're lucky."

"Hey," Jimmy said, looking at the window behind them. "Someone just drove up."

"Probably one of the band," Jet said. "Gus said he was going to town."

"It's not a truck. It's a—hey, I think that's Jason's car!"

Grace turned and looked out the windows as the headlights of a small car went dark. She couldn't see much in the darkness, but two car doors slammed shut and the three McLintocks rushed out of the living room door.

8

"I TOLD YOU I WAS bringing a surprise." Jason, the tallest and thinnest McLintock brother, introduced his family to the tall, slender woman by his side. "I'd like you to meet Anne Carter, my fiancée."

"Fiancée?" Jack echoed, exchanging a quick look of concern with Grace. He was sure she was thinking the same thing he was. Another complication. A big one. *"Fiancée?"*

"Yep," Jason said, a worried look in his eyes. "I wanted it to be a surprise. I mean, I thought you guys would be happy for me."

"Hi," Grace said, shaking the young woman's hand. "I'm Grace Daniels, a friend of Jack's, from Dallas."

"No kidding?"

"Of course we're happy for you. That's great," Jack said to Jason, managing to hide his surprise and give his brother a hug. Then he turned to Anne. "It's our pleasure to meet you. And we're happy to welcome you to the family."

Jason took Anne's hand and led her over to Isabella, who had stayed in the rocking chair while she cradled the sleeping child.

"Welcome home, honey," the old woman said. "It's been too long."

"Bella, I'm going to get married in a few weeks."

"That is wonderful." She patted Jason's cheek as he bent to kiss her, then she took Anne's hand. "We had no idea!"

"I thought he should have warned you," Anne said.

"Who's the baby?"

"Shh," Anne told her future husband. "You'll wake him up."

"He belongs to Grace," Bella said. "His name is Mac."

"Hi, Mac," Jason said, keeping his voice low this time. He looked at Bella. "Does he ever wake up and play?"

"Yes, and then you have to fight your older brothers to get near him."

Anne touched the baby's hair with one finger. "He's so sweet," she murmured.

"So, you're really engaged?" Jet asked.

Jimmy smacked his youngest brother on the back. "I can't believe it. You?"

"Hey," Jason protested. "I'm twenty-one as of Friday, and I'm going to England for two years. We decided not to wait." He looked over to his older brother. "You don't think it's a bad idea, do you, Jack?"

He opened his mouth, then closed it again. He sure as hell didn't know what kind of an idea it was. "I'm glad you brought Anne home for the party," he managed to say. "I'm a little surprised by this whole marriage idea, though, but I'm sure we'll have a chance to talk about your plans in the next few days." He took Anne's hand. "It's a pleasure to meet you, Anne. I hope this bunch of cowboys doesn't make you crazy. And welcome to the family." And please, he added silently, be an understanding woman if your future husband is already a father. He'd seen the tender look she'd given Max. It could be worse. The young couple would have a nice nest egg once the Freemont money was released, Jason had his future ahead of him, and Anne seemed to like babies. Maybe, just maybe, there was hope.

Now all he had to do was pray that his youngest brother had had sex with a redhead in Dallas.

It was a strange prayer, Jack thought later, long after everyone else had gone to bed and he sat alone in the living room. But it sure as hell beat the alternative.

GRACE FIXED MAC'S MORNING bottle when the kitchen was empty and tiptoed back to her room to feed the baby in private. She didn't want to face the rest of the family right away. In fact, she wanted to stall for as long as she possibly could. She needed time to decide what to do next.

"I think it's time to leave," she told the baby, who fixed his brown-eyed gaze on her as he sucked down his breakfast. "I tried, sweetheart, but I'll be darned if I can figure out who your father is."

She gazed out the long windows to the courtyard. Yellow flowers in brightly colored pots lined the perimeter now. She and Isabella had made a lot of progress by working together the past few mornings, while it was still cool enough to weed and plant. They were ready for that party, if Isabella's cooking frenzy was any indication. Jason would celebrate in style, while she would take Mac and return to Dallas.

Jason wasn't involved, not that she could tell. That nice young man with his nice young fiancée couldn't possibly have had a weekend affair with Lucy. He was too young, for one thing. And even if he had, would Anne be willing to mother a child who wasn't hers?

Maybe or maybe not, but Grace had begun to wonder if what she'd thought was the right thing for Mac wasn't the right thing at all. She'd wanted to give him a father, a family of his own. She'd wanted him to grow up knowing where he belonged, but so far she hadn't been able to discover where that was. So she would take Mac and leave the McLintocks to their celebration and their reunion and their dreams of fame and fortune.

"Saturday already. We've been here a week," she told the baby, lifting him to a sitting position. "You're getting a tooth and learning how to sit in a high chair, and I've ridden a horse and been to a country-western bar. Haven't we had an exciting time?"

Mac smiled at her, drool escaping from his bottom lip and sliding past the cleft in his chin.

"But I don't know if we should still be here. Maybe I should have let the lawyers sort everything out from the beginning." She wiped Mac's distinctive chin with a tissue. "I guess it was pretty dumb of me to think I could take care of this myself."

Mac grabbed for the tissue and managed to rip a small section and put it into his mouth. Grace fished it out and wiped his damp chin one more time. "I guess you're stuck with Auntie Grace for a while longer, sweetheart." She gathered him into her arms and walked over to the window. "At least until I can decide what to do."

The baby patted the glass and chuckled. He wanted to touch everything he saw lately. The world was an exciting place when you were discovering it for the first time. "Window," Grace told him. "And see the pretty flowers out there?"

He patted the window again and left a sticky handprint on the glass. "Uh-oh," she said, making him smile. "Guess who will be cleaning a window today? Come on," she said, opening the door to the courtyard. They would take the shortcut to the kitchen. Perhaps she would see Jack. If he had some answers from Jason, then the two of them could sit down and make a decision about Mac's future.

And then she would leave. It was time. If she stayed any longer, she risked falling in love with cowboys and ranches and courtyards. It meant hoping that a handsome rancher would kiss her good-night and smile at her in the morning. She couldn't keep her heart safe much longer.

"HAVE YOU STARTED drinking?" Jason asked, giving Jack an odd look. "It's only nine in the morning."

"Lucy Bagwell," Jack repeated. "Did you have an affair with her in Dallas a year ago last March?"

Jason smiled. "This is a trick, right? Jet put you up to it, didn't he?"

"Look," Jack said, praying for patience as he sank

into his office chair. He'd managed to pry Jason away from his exuberant brothers and his quiet fiancée this morning, and now the darn kid thought he was playing a joke on him. "A lot is at stake here, Jay, and I'm not playing games. You saw that little boy last night?"

"Yeah. Cute kid."

"Well, he's got 'McLintock' on his birth certificate and none of us know how it got there."

"And you think it's *me?*" Jason turned red all the way to the tips of his ears. "You think I'm his father?"

"It has occurred to me, yes."

"Heck, Jack, I'm not doing stuff like that. I'm engaged to be married."

"I'm talking about fifteen months ago, not now."

"Fifteen months ago I was up to my neck in English Lit classes. I wasn't in Dallas having, uh, you know. I sure wasn't making babies."

Jack leaned forward and made sure that Jason looked him in the eye. "If there ever was a time to tell the truth, Jason, this is it."

The boy didn't flinch. "It couldn't be me."

"You're positive? I have to be sure."

Jason turned even redder, but he held Jack's gaze with a steady look. "I've never, uh, done it."

Oh, shit. "Never?"

Jason shook his head. "I came close a few times, but nope—never. With all the talk of disease and everything, I never found a woman who was worth it."

"You don't have to be embarrassed," Jack said. "You made some safe decisions. But you and Anne haven't, uh, slept together, either?"

"We decided to wait until after we were married."
He grinned. "Which is why we decided to get married.
It's getting harder and harder to stay apart."

"Yeah," Jack said, thinking of living here in the
house with Grace for the past week. He'd watched her
walk and smile, he'd smelled her cologne and he'd listened to her laugh and he'd wanted to kiss her so badly
that he'd had to excuse himself and go out to the barn
and hide. "I understand."

"Anne wanted to go to England, too, because she
was a history major, so we thought it would work out
better this way, getting married and all."

"And I'm sure it will." He hesitated, wondering the
best way to phrase his next question. "Have you told
anyone about, uh, this part of your life?"

"You mean my brothers?"

"Yes, that's exactly who I mean."

Jason made a face. "Hell, no. They'd rib me until I
fell over into the dust."

"Let's keep it between us for now, until I figure out
what to do about Mac."

"Whose son is he, then?"

"I don't think he belongs to any of us. There must
have been a mistake," Jack assured him. "I talked to
Artie on Monday, and he's going to look into it for
me."

"Good. I didn't figure that Jet or Jimmy would do
something like that."

"But what if they didn't know there was a baby?
Those things happen."

Jason shrugged. "Which is another good reason for

me to, well, you know, but I'll be real glad after the wedding's over."

"And when is the wedding going to take place?"

"In a few weeks. We're still trying to figure it out."

Jack stood up and held out his hand. "I don't know if I had a chance to say it last night, but congratulations."

Jason took Jack's hand and smiled. "Grandpa Freemont's money is going to come in handy. You guys have waited a long time for me to be twenty-one."

"I was congratulating you on your upcoming wedding."

"And I'm congratulating *us* on making it through. I know it wasn't easy."

"No," Jack said, releasing his young brother's hand. "But it was sure worth it."

He meant it, too. He sat in his chair long after Jason had gone to find his future bride and take her for a ride around part of the ranch. He hoped they would end up kissing in the barn. Which was something he wouldn't mind doing, either, come to think of it. With Grace.

And Grace hadn't seemed to mind when he'd kissed her by the stream that day. She'd kissed him back, an encouraging reaction. He'd had all he could do to get on his horse and lead her back home.

Jack leaned back in his chair and closed his eyes. If he were free to do whatever he wanted, he'd take Grace to bed. He wouldn't worry about who Mac's father was, or wonder in what part of Texas old J.T. was causing trouble. He'd let all the boys go off on their adventures, he'd pay off the bank loans, he'd admire the sunset, and then go make love to Grace.

He'd be a satisfied man, yes, sir.

Oh, Lord, how he wished the next few days would pass quickly. There were too many secrets for one cowboy to keep track of. He wished he could stop being a brother and simply act like a man who wanted one particular woman, but now he had to tell her that Jason wasn't Mac's father.

And she would want to know who was, he wouldn't be able to tell her, and she would leave. Jack paused in the living room and remembered when Grace had stood there and told him in no uncertain terms that she was bringing Mac to his father.

If Mac's father was an aging, hot-tempered cowboy with a taste for women and whiskey, a man with more wanderlust than common sense, what then? Would she give that boy to him, anyway?

He couldn't take the chance. Damn it, he didn't want her to leave. He wanted a date for his own party. He wanted someone to dance with and someone to talk to. Someone special. Someone like Grace.

Jet or Jimmy would know how to convince her to stay. They knew what to say to women, how to behave. One of them would have to tell him what to do.

"YOU MIGHT SMILE MORE often," Jet said, restringing his guitar. "Women like it when you smile at them."

"I don't know about that." Jimmy shook his head. "I think women like that brooding look. You know, like you have dark secrets and pain. They always fall for a man who looks like he's in pain."

"Pain?" Jack clearly didn't get it. "I could do the

'dark secret' thing, but I'm not real sure about the pain."

Jet grinned. Old Jack was finally starting to notice that there was a beautiful woman in the house. "You have some dark secrets, Jack? You keeping something from us?"

"Another thing, Jack. You've got to spend some time with her."

"I work all the goddamn day."

"Jet and I have been doing some of your chores. Didn't you notice?"

"Yeah, but I thought you were trying to get caught up before you left."

Jimmy sighed dramatically and rolled his eyes at Jet. "I told you he wouldn't notice."

"We were trying to give you more time. Time to spend with Grace."

Jimmy nodded. "Jet figured you're going to be lonely after we leave, and having Grace around would help."

"Lonely?" Jack roared. "You make me sound like some old retired geezer. I'm only thirty-six and I have a life."

Jet set his guitar aside. "Okay, Jack. Tell us about your life. When's the last time you had a date? Before Grace came, that is."

"I don't remember."

"It was the librarian," Jimmy pointed out. "A year ago? Didn't you take her to see me in *Fiddler on the Roof*?"

"Not one of your better performances, either," his oldest brother pointed out.

"You think it's easy dancing like that?"

Jet held up his hands. "Okay, so maybe we'd better not talk about the past. Have you kissed Grace yet?"

"That's none of your damn b—"

"He has," Jimmy declared, nodding toward Jet.

"How do you know that?"

"He almost smiled. Means he's kissed her. Probably a couple of times, right, Jack?"

"Well, I don't think it's right to talk about—"

"You're not down at the Stampede, Jack. You're in the slaughterhouse with your brothers. You asked our advice. We're giving it to you." Jet tried not to laugh, but it wasn't easy to keep a straight face when his older brother looked so confused. "Spend some more time with her, Jack. Take her riding. Or take the truck and go have a picnic. Women love picnics, and you'll have the built-in advantage of lying on a blanket with her, and the whole time she'll think you're being sensitive."

"Why?"

"Why what?" Jet picked up his guitar and tested the new strings. It would be kind of fun to write a song about picnics and sex, something upbeat for dancing.

"Why do they think you're sensitive if you're eating on a blanket?"

Jet shrugged. "Beats me."

Jack turned to Jimmy, who didn't look any more enlightened. "I don't know, either, but I agree with Jet. Have Bella fix a lunch for you. Women are always happy if you're feeding them."

Jack didn't look convinced, but Jet figured it was sinking in somewhere in his brother's thick skull. "One more thing," Jet said. "It's about time you stopped worrying about that baby and started wondering how to impress the lady. Everything else will take care of itself."

"I wish you were right," Jack said.

Jimmy nodded. "Good, Jack. You've got that 'dark secret-pain' look down perfect."

"Have you seen her anywhere?"

Jet nodded. "She was here a few minutes ago. She said something about going back to Dallas." He watched his older brother turn pale.

"When?"

"About half an hour ago."

"No, I meant when did she say she was leaving?"

Jet shrugged. "I don't know. I've offered to teach her a song, so she might come back when we rehearse. If Lina's girls will watch Mac while he takes a nap."

"Teach her a song?" Jack repeated, as if he couldn't believe it. "Grace?"

"Yeah. She was real surprised when I asked her, but then she said okay. But she said she was leaving, so she didn't know if she'd have time."

"She's not leaving," Jack said. "Not until after Jason's birthday."

Jimmy cleared his throat. "Is he, uh, you know, Mac's father?"

The guys in the band walked in the door, so Jack stood up to leave. "We'll talk about that Friday. If you see Grace, tell her I'm looking for her."

"My pleasure," Jet said, nodding. Jack was going to do just fine. He picked up his guitar and looked at Gus. "You guys ready to rock and roll?"

"WHERE THE HELL IS SHE?"

Isabella didn't turn around but continued to mix batter in a huge bowl. "Who?"

"Grace, of course." Jack leaned against the counter and waited for Bella to give him an answer. "I've looked all over the house."

"She went outside with the baby."

"And where did she go?"

"I don't know. Perhaps to visit Lina. The girls were here earlier wanting to know if they could have Mac for a while." She looked over and smiled. "He is a sweet boy. The girls love him. We're keeping him, aren't we?"

"No. I don't know."

"He's not Jason's child, then."

Jack debated whether or not to tell her about Jason's denial, then decided against it. "I don't know yet."

"You are the only one who was in Dallas that month," Bella declared. "The others are not his father."

"And neither am I."

The old woman went back to stirring the cake batter.

"Go ahead," Jack said. "Say whatever it is you're thinking."

"No." She shook her head and rested the spoon against the side of the bowl. "I think I will be very quiet and pretend to know nothing. Like you."

Jack turned away. "I'm going to keep looking."

"You're in a hurry to find her?"

"I thought she might want to go on a, uh, picnic."

Bella chuckled. "I will fix you something to take with you. She is a pretty lady, and very kind, too. Maybe you should think about settling down."

He looked over his shoulder to see the old woman laughing at him. "I've lived on this ranch all of my life. How much more settled could a man get?"

"Oh, it takes a woman to settle a man," Bella said. "Didn't you know that?"

Jack kept walking. He didn't figure that deserved an answer. He'd been unsettled since Grace Daniels walked into his life.

"Try the courtyard," Isabella called. "She's usually out there in the morning."

Jack didn't point out that it was almost lunchtime. He'd tried the courtyard before, but it had been frustratingly empty except for all of those flowers in their pots. The courtyard had looked ready for the party. He wished he felt ready for a party. He heard the Naked Ladies start practicing in the slaughterhouse, which meant they were getting ready for the party, too. Jet had promised they wouldn't practice late at night and disturb Lina and Ed, so they'd adjusted their hours to something closer to normal.

If you could call a group of guys who named themselves the Naked Ladies normal.

She was there, in the courtyard where Bella said she would be. She wore white shorts and a shirt the color of the bright flowers she touched with her fingertips. He watched her and she didn't know it, and he wondered once again if the surge of longing that filled him was simple loneliness or something else. His brothers said he was lonely; he didn't feel lonely. Or at least he hadn't felt lonely until Grace arrived and he'd realized that he was indeed alone. Even in a house filled with noisy brothers.

Which didn't make sense.

Bella would tell him that things didn't have to make sense, that sometimes things just are the way they are.

He wanted to take her riding. He wanted to see her smile, and he wanted to kiss her again. He needed to make her stay. There was no telling what would happen when she returned to Dallas and called a lawyer. She had six days to stir up trouble; he had six days to prevent it. But lawyers and paternity suits fled his mind as Grace looked up and saw him in the doorway. Her smile warmed him, and he smiled, an idiot smile, in return. He opened the door and walked outside, across the courtyard to the woman who stopped touching flowers and put her hands in her pockets as he approached her.

"The courtyard looks good," he said. "Bella said the two of you have been working hard."

"I enjoyed it."

"And so did Bella."

"I thought you were working," she said. "You're not riding the range today?"

"Not yet. I came to ask you if you wanted to go with me. Bella will fix us a lunch."

She hesitated. "I don't think I should be going anywhere but back to Dallas, Jack. I've been here too long with nothing settled. I have to go back and find a home for Mac."

"Come riding with me," he urged. "We'll talk about it."

Grace didn't budge. "Jason and Anne have Mac, but I don't know how long they're willing to watch him."

"You go change into your riding clothes and I'll find out."

"Jason's not his father, is he?"

"We'll talk about it later, all right?"

"All right." She took her hands out of her pockets and swept her hair from her face. "Do I get to ride that nice, slow horse again?"

"I'll saddle him myself," Jack assured her. "I'll meet you at the barn in thirty minutes. Do you still have the hat I loaned you?"

"Yes."

"Good." He hesitated, then turned away. She'd said she'd go with him. At least he'd gotten that far.

THIS WOULD BE THE LAST day, she promised herself. Her last day at the ranch, her last day with Jack. She planned to enjoy herself, without a repeat of the embarrassing kiss they'd shared last time they'd gone for a ride. This would be strictly business, a private lunch to discuss what would happen to Mac. They were two adults who should be able to come up with an acceptable plan.

Just because he was handsome and looked about as sexy as a man could get in those jeans and boots didn't mean a thing. She would keep her mind on business and babies and the important things in life. They rode for more than an hour. The ever-present breeze kept Grace from feeling the afternoon heat. He stopped before a grove of trees nestled near a shallow watering hole. Several head of cattle lazed in the heat and looked at them with curious brown eyes as they dismounted.

He came over to help her from her horse, barely touching her waist to make sure she didn't fall. This time her feet held her up, so she turned around to tell him that she was getting used to riding, after all. One minute she was looking up at him and the next she was in his arms. She didn't intend to put her arms around him, but he bent to kiss her, and she didn't stop to think that she shouldn't be kissing him, or anyone, really. She should be back at the ranch packing up her car and saying goodbye to everyone.

Her hat fell to the ground. His hands gripped her waist and held her to him while his mouth tasted hers. It was the kind of kiss that made her forget where she was. She wanted to sink to the ground and have him follow her down, but he held her upright and kissed her neck, the sensitive skin below her earlobe, the hollow at the base of her throat, before returning to her lips. His tongue teased hers, made her cling to him even harder. After long moments, during which Grace figured she would gladly spend the rest of her life kissing this man, he lifted his lips from hers and caught his breath.

"Oh, hell," he muttered, and kissed her again. Then he scooped her into his arms and carried her to the shade. Grace wrapped her arms around his neck and hung on.

"Why are you swearing?"

"Because," he said, setting her carefully on the dry grass, "I was going to wait until after lunch to kiss you."

She smiled. "I thought we were going to talk about Mac."

He sat beside her and leaned against the tree. Their thighs touched, turning Grace's skin warm. "I lied."

"I didn't think a McLintock ever lied," she couldn't help teasing.

"I did, this one time," he admitted. "To get you to come out with me. Jet told me that women like picnics, so I figured I'd give it a try."

She smiled at him. "So far, so good."

He leaned over and kissed her on the lips. Their embrace began simply and ended with half of Grace's clothes unbuttoned and Jack lying on top of her. It was a few minutes before either one of them could speak.

"I guess I'd better get the food." He stood up and walked over to the horses and retrieved the saddlebags. He returned to the base of the tree and spread out a large cloth, then placed plastic containers and silverware in the middle. "There," he said. "Bella packed enough stuff for five cowhands."

"Should I start opening them?"

"Yeah. I'll pour us something cold to drink." He sat down, rummaged through the bag and found two tin cups and a bottle of wine. He fiddled with a Swiss Army knife and found the corkscrew, uncorked the bottle and poured them each a glass of wine. "Now, this is what I call living."

The containers held shredded lettuce, chopped vegetables, cheese, sliced grilled chicken breasts and homemade corn tortillas. "You don't usually have tacos on Saturday afternoons?"

"No, Grace." He handed her a cup. "But I'm not complaining."

"Neither am I." She took a sip of the white wine and then looked down at the food in front of them. "Bella went to a lot of trouble."

"She likes you." He took paper plates from the other bag, then rummaged to the bottom and found paper napkins.

"I like her, too. She's been very kind to me, and she treats Mac like one of her own grandchildren."

"Then, why are you talking about leaving?"

"It's time."

"Nothing's been decided."

"Exactly," Grace said. "Nothing's been decided and nothing is going to be. It's time I went home. I probably should have never come here in the first place. Jason's not Mac's father, and the rest of you deny knowing Lucy."

"We've told you the truth," he insisted, but she noticed he didn't look at her when he said the words. "Stay," he said, lifting his gaze to hers. "Why don't you stay and be my date for next weekend?"

Don't fall in love with a cowboy, Gracie. Grace ignored the words of advice echoing in her head. If she stopped to think about it she'd probably have to admit it was too late. "I'd like that."

"Good. Do you think we could pretend that we're just two people who have gone out to lunch?" He looked down at the food spread between them and handed her a paper plate.

Considering the way she'd kissed him, Grace wondered if she was capable of pretending anything. "Yes," she said, hoping for the best. "I think that's a good idea."

He smiled, and Grace wished he'd kiss her again. Tacos were tempting, but kissing this particular cowboy was much better. She took the plate and concentrated on food.

9

"STAND HERE AND SING into the microphone."

"I can't sing," Grace said, standing where Jet told her to stand. The slaughterhouse was a strange building, with large hooks hanging from the ceiling and stains on the cement floor. It certainly didn't look like a great place to break into song.

"Sure you can," he insisted. "Just sing 'Take off your boots' whenever I point to you and Gus. Jack, too. You're the chorus."

"I've never been in a chorus," she said, just so he'd know she had no experience singing alone or in a group. She'd been so shy as a teenager that she'd been afraid to sing along with the songs on the radio for fear someone would listen and make fun of her. She hadn't felt like singing much in those days, either.

"You are now," he said, and waved Jack over. "Jack, come on over here. Stand beside Grace and get ready to sing 'Take off your boots' when the time comes."

Jack stepped over to Grace's side. "This must be a new song."

"Yeah. I wrote it this morning, and I'm real anxious to hear how it's going to sound." He tried out a few chords on the guitar. "I think this is the right key," he muttered, then turned around to the band. "It's fast, but it should have a pretty good beat. You guys all set?'' They nodded. "One-two-three!"

The crash of chords made Grace jump, and Jack touched her back to steady her and smiled. It was too loud to try to talk to him, so she smiled back as he took her hand. Jet started singing about a man who couldn't find love and how sad he was about being alone.

Jack cleared his throat.

Jet winked, then launched into what Grace figured was the chorus. "Take off your boots!"

"Take off your boots," Grace echoed, along with Jack. He had a surprisingly mellow baritone.

"Come over here and see me," Jet crooned. "Take off your boots!"

Grace was ready. "Take off your boots!" she sang, louder this time.

"I've got a little more to say, so take off your boots," Jet sang, then pointed.

"Take off your boots," they sang.

"Come a little bit closer."

"Take off your boots!"

"I'm never goin' away."

Grace stepped back from the microphone and laughed. Jet winked at her, continued with the second verse and nodded to the drummer. She couldn't believe she'd just sung a country-western song with the man who'd written it. She couldn't believe that Jack had sung along with her.

Jack nudged her. "Take off your boots," he sang near her ear. Grace joined in as quickly as she could.

She didn't know how this weekend could get any

better. Yesterday afternoon had been the picnic. And the kissing. She'd spent Saturday night in the midst of the family, with Jet playing his guitar and singing everyone's requests. This morning Grace and Mac had slept late. She had awakened to hear Mac gurgling and cooing in his bed. She'd heard the comforting sound of someone watering plants in the courtyard and muffled laughter in the hall. Now it was Sunday and she was singing with a band.

And Jack was still holding her hand. "Take off your boots," she sang, right on cue this time.

She was really starting to have a good time.

"WHAT'S THE MATTER with him?" Jason ruffled Mac's hair as the baby sat screaming in the high chair, but the child refused to be distracted.

"I think he's getting a tooth. That's what Grace says," Jack answered.

Jason grinned. "Well, if Grace said it, it must be right."

"What's that supposed to mean?"

His youngest brother chuckled. "Nothing. Where'd she go?"

"To her room to get something for Mac." Jack looked at his watch. It was after two, and Isabella had promised she'd give him a list that he could take to town. She knew he usually went to town on Mondays, and this was supposed to be a major shopping trip. He'd hoped to talk Grace into going with him, but if something was wrong with Mac, Jack knew she wouldn't be able to leave him.

"If you're going to stay with him, then I'll go out and help Jet with the horses. Isabella went over to Lina's for a few minutes."

"Go ahead. I need to talk to Grace, anyway," Jack said as Jason grabbed his hat and hurried from the kitchen.

"Come here, kid." Jack lifted Mac from his chair and held him in his arms so the child, now a little quieter, could look around the room. The phone rang, and Jack answered it. "McLintocks," he said.

"Jack?"

"Yeah." The baby tugged at the cord.

"This is Artie. Can you talk?"

"Not exactly," he replied, watching Grace step into the kitchen. She smiled when she saw the baby in his arms. "Just a minute," he told the lawyer, and managed to hand Mac to Grace without dropping him or the telephone receiver. He spoke into the phone. "But I'm coming into town this afternoon. How about if we get together later?"

"Good." The man sounded relieved. "I'll be free any time after four."

"I'll be there." Jack hesitated. "This is important?"

"I wouldn't have called you otherwise, Jack. Did you have any luck talking to Jason?"

"No."

"I was afraid of that. See you later."

"Yeah. Thanks." He hung up the phone and took a deep breath before plastering a stupid smile on his face. *Did you find him* was what he'd wanted to ask, but he couldn't, not with Grace fussing over Mac a couple of feet away.

Grace looked over to him. "Is something wrong?"

"No. I just have some business to take care of in town."

"I heard you were going to pick up supplies. Would you mind getting Mac some more formula? I'll pay—"

"Don't worry about it." He could certainly afford to feed his nephew. Or his brother. Jack studied Mac's now-familiar face. *Brother?* "Just write down the name so I get the right kind."

"Okay. Thanks." She hesitated. "Would you like some help with the groceries? Mac's pretty good in the car."

And take the chance that he'd be recognized? No way. "No, I'm fine," he said, a little harsher than he intended. He tried to smile, but he could tell by the look on her face that he didn't look like he was smiling. "But thanks for offering," he said. "I have some business in town to take care of, and I don't know how long it will take."

"Okay. I just thought I'd ask." She busied herself putting medicine on Mac's gums while he fussed and drooled.

He had five days. Four, really, if he didn't count Friday. Friday morning at nine-thirty the four McLintock brothers would be standing in the office of Locklin Federal Savings Bank while the trustees wrote out checks for large sums of money.

If there were five McLintocks, no one would get a

dime. And it would be J.T.'s fault, of course. Most things were.

"HE'S STILL ALIVE, all right." Artie handed Jack a manila file. "Read it and weep."

Jack sat down and opened the file while Artie poured whiskey into two glasses and put one on the desk in front of Jack. Instead of sitting behind his desk, he sat beside Jack in the vacant leather chair. "He's living in El Paso," Jack said. "The rumors were right."

"When's the last time you heard from him?"

"Oh, it's been years. I told him he was welcome to stay if he wanted to work for me." Jack took a sip of his drink. "He didn't, so he left." He turned the page to see a detailed description of J.T.'s whereabouts the past three years. "How the hell did you get all this?"

Artie shrugged. "I hired the best. Turn to page two. That's where it all hits the fan."

Jack turned the page. It was easy to see, about a third of the way down the page. "He was in Dallas during the winter Mac was conceived."

"Yep. He had a job there, but it didn't work out. So he went back to El Paso. Alone. There are some copies of interviews conducted with the people he worked with in El Paso, also interviews with three women and one man who worked with Lucy Bagwell. Nothing unusual, and they all expressed sympathy for Lucy's death."

"So another nice lady was conned by J.T."

"Looks like it. If you're sure none of your brothers is responsible."

Jack took another drink of the whiskey, then another. "I guess I'm as sure as I'm going to get."

Artie shook his head. "Damn shame."

Jack took the folder and placed it on Artie's desk. "Now what?"

"You take that folder out of the office, for one thing. This was a private matter."

"All right. And what about the child?"

"That's up to you. You and your brothers are going to be rich men on Friday morning. As soon as all of the 'McLintock boys' have turned twenty-one."

"Chances are that Mac is one of the boys."

"And he's not even a year old. You want to wait another twenty years for your money?" Artie got up and returned with the whiskey bottle while Jack debated how to answer that question.

"I'd be lying if I said I wanted to wait. But I don't want to do anything illegal. Especially if Mac is my brother. Would I be lying by letting the trust money be disbursed on Friday?"

"Not necessarily. You don't know for sure who Mac's father is. You don't even know if he's J.T.'s kid. You'd have to find your father and have DNA tests to be positive. That could take months, even years. Does the woman who brought him here have any legal rights?"

"Not that I know of."

"Then the state of Texas would have to get involved, but I doubt if they'd go to the trouble and the expense. They'll most likely declare him a ward of the court and see about getting him adopted."

"Which I could do myself."

Artie shook his head and poured some more whiskey. "Not without some claim to him. And why would you want to take care of a baby, anyway?"

"If he's one of the family—"

"Pretty big 'if,'" the lawyer pointed out. "And it would open up a pretty big can of worms."

Jack leaned back in the chair. "I wish it was Friday."

"You and me both. You're going to lose the ranch if you don't pay off those loans. I'd hate to see everything you've worked for go up in smoke."

"Yeah," Jack said. "Me, too."

"I'm going to assume the woman and the baby are still with you."

Jack nodded. "Fortunately. She wanted to leave, but I talked her into staying."

"Good." Artie sat back in his chair. "If you can keep things quiet for a few more days, I think you'll get through this just fine."

"Yeah," Jack agreed, but he wished he was miles away from Locklin right now. He didn't like being in the middle, and he wasn't much for subterfuge. He wanted to explain the trust fund to Grace, but she was so damned insistent on Mac having a father that she'd probably deliver the child to J.T. in El Paso. And that was the last thing the little fellow deserved.

No, he'd have to keep his mouth shut for the time being. He'd get the money and pay off the ranch. The boys would take theirs and follow their dreams. Everyone would get what they deserved.

Except Mac. If the kid was really a McLintock, he was coming out of this with the short end of the stick.

Jack took another swallow of the whiskey, which had begun to warm his insides. If he didn't take his inheritance, the only thing he could offer Mac was a debt-ridden ranch and a good bunch of calves.

"BUT HOW DO YOU WRITE a song like that?" Grace sat outside in the evening shade at the edge of the courtyard and watched Jet water the flowers. Mac lay on the blanket beside her, his bare feet kicking hers. "Where do you get your ideas?"

Jet turned off the water and flopped down on the blanket near Mac. "They just come to me. Sometimes Jason sends me lyrics, and all I have to do is put them to music."

"He sends you his poetry?"

"Sometimes. I have some real nice slow songs that we're working on now. Nice ballads, which aren't exactly my style." He smiled that devastating smile. "I'm a honky-tonk man, but it doesn't hurt to have a few belly-rubbin' songs for the ladies."

"Belly-rubbing?"

"Yeah. You know. Slow songs."

Grace laughed. The young man was outrageous. "I've never heard that phrase."

"Now, why doesn't that surprise me?" He tickled Mac's bare belly. "I wish I was that little again, so I could just lie around in my underwear and stare at pretty flowers."

"Your mother must have had her hands full with

four boys. I can barely manage one boy for a few weeks."

Jet's smile faded. "Our mother worked hard, that's for sure. I don't know what any of us would have done without Jack. He was older than the rest of us, and we looked up to him. He always had all the answers."

"He seems like the kind of man who will always be there," Grace said, touched by Jet's obvious love for his older brother.

"Yeah. He's that kind of guy." He looked at his watch. "He should have been back by now. It's not like Jack to miss supper."

"He had errands in town."

Jet frowned. "He shouldn't be this late. It's starting to get dark."

"And time for me to put Mac to bed," Grace said, scooping Mac into her arms. She grabbed his blanket with her free hand and stood up.

"I wonder where Jack could be," Jet muttered. "The boys and I are going to San Antonio to meet a friend of Gus's who spent a couple of years in Nashville. Will you tell Jack that we might just spend the night there if it gets late?"

"Sure." She hoped she'd see Jack tonight, though he'd been aloof this afternoon. He hadn't wanted company when he went to town, that was certain. He hadn't even said goodbye. Grace told herself it was foolish to be disappointed. "Are you leaving now?"

"Yeah." He looked at his watch again. "And I'm late. You need any help before I take off?"

"No, but thanks."

"Did Jase go to the movies?"

"He and Anne left a while ago." She held Mac up for Jet to kiss good-night. "Have a good time in San Antonio."

"Thanks." He hurried through the courtyard and out of one of the side doors. Grace made her way to the kitchen to get Mac's evening bottle. He started to fuss when she took it from the refrigerator. He was still fussing when she ran hot water over the bottle and the phone began to ring. He fussed while she turned the water off and reached for the telephone.

"McLintocks," she said, imitating the way Jack answered the phone.

"Hey, honey, could one of you come out here and pick up Jack? He's here at the Stampede, and he can't exactly drive himself home tonight." The man's voice was almost drowned out by country-western music and conversation.

"Excuse me, but who is this?" She wondered if it could be a joke that one of the boys was playing on her.

"Ed Burley. You want to send Jet or someone to get his brother?"

"Sure. Thank you very much for calling."

"Yeah. Just come get him out of here before he causes any trouble."

Grace hung up the phone and, still holding Mac in her arms, gave the baby his bottle while she looked out the window for Jet. She couldn't see the Naked Ladies bus, so she walked through the house to the living room in time to see a cloud of dust swirling around the back of the bus as it lumbered down the driveway.

"Darn," she said softly, and almost jumped out of her skin when a man spoke.

"You need help, Grace?"

She turned to see Jimmy in a corner chair with a thick sheaf of papers on his lap. "A man just called from the Stampede and wants someone to go get Jack."

Jimmy looked confused. "Get Jack?"

"It seems he's had too much to drink and they don't think he should drive home."

"Get Jack?" Jimmy repeated. "No one's ever had to get Jack. He hardly ever drinks. Doesn't approve."

Grace adjusted her grip on the baby, took the empty bottle out of his mouth and lifted him to her shoulder. "That's what the man—a Mr. Burley—said. I was trying to catch Jet before he left, but I missed him. Jason and Anne went to the movies."

"Yeah. They sure are cute together."

Grace smiled. "Yes, they sure are. Can you get Jack?"

"Sure, I'll—" He stopped, then cleared his throat. "Oh, shoot, Gracie. No, never mind." He rose from his chair and put the manuscript on the floor. "I'll do it."

"What's the matter?"

"Nothing."

But she could tell something was wrong. "Were you leaving, too?"

"I was waiting for a call to discuss this project," he admitted, pointing to the thick stack of paper. "It's something I hope to audition for in L.A."

Grace hesitated. "Is there anyone else who can go?"

"Nope. Unless you could help me out?" He reached

for Mac and gently took the child into his arms. "I could stay here and read some stories to Mac until he went to sleep."

"Well, I—"

"Do you know where the Stampede is?"

"I was there once, but I don't—"

"It's on the highway. Turn left when you leave the ranch, like you're heading to town. Just stay on the road for about thirty miles and it's on the west corner of the first intersection."

"That sounds easy enough." She watched as Mac lay his head on Jimmy-Joe's shoulder. "And Mac's tired. He should go to sleep without much trouble."

"He's never any trouble," the young man assured her. "He's a good little guy." Jimmy flashed that charming smile. "You go get Jack and don't worry about a thing."

"I'm not sure I can handle this," Grace said, still uncertain.

"There's no one else," Jimmy insisted. "And you're just the person to talk to Jack and find out why he's sitting alone in a bar on a Monday night."

"Why me?"

Jimmy gave her a wink and pushed her gently toward the hall. "Because, sweetheart, you're probably the reason he's there."

JACK BLINKED AGAINST the sight before him. Grace Daniels, her gray eyes worried and her sweet, rosy lips curved into the gentlest of frowns, stood before him in that flowery dress. Once again she looked out of place, but he felt a strange sense of comfort at the sight of her. And the immediate stirring of pure lust.

"What the hell are you doing here?"

She sat down on the bar stool next to him, set her car keys on the counter and swiveled in his direction. "I've come to take you home."

"How did you know I was here?"

"Mr. Burley called me and said you couldn't drive and that someone should come get you."

Jack looked at the empty glass that sat in front of him. He'd asked Burley to call home for him, but he hadn't expected Grace to show up. "It's not that I can't drive. A friend of mine brought me here. My truck is still parked in town."

"He left you here all by yourself?"

"I insisted." He'd insisted on feeling sorry for himself. Now all he felt was empty. And alone.

"Well, I'm glad you did."

The bartender wiped the counter in front of Grace and asked her if she wanted anything.

"No, thank you," she said in that soft voice of hers. The man looked as if he wanted to stay and talk to her, but Jack gave him a dirty look that sent him looking for another customer. "You don't look drunk," she said, studying his face.

"I'm not." All he had to do was look at her and he felt dizzy. It wasn't whiskey causing his problems.

"Mr. Burley said you couldn't drive home."

"I told you, my truck is in town. I asked Burley to call home and see if anyone was coming into town who could give me a lift. I didn't think they'd send you. Who's taking care of Mac?"

"Jimmy. He volunteered because he had to stay home and wait for a phone call from Los Angeles."

"Yeah, I'll bet he did." Jimmy-Joe was matchmaking as much as Jet was. "I'm just surprised they sent you."

"No one else could do it." She picked up her keys and slid off the stool. "Shall we go get your truck, then?"

"No."

She returned that cute little bottom to the stool.

"Why not?" she asked.

"You can drive me home," he said, reluctant to let her out of his sight. "After we have a dance."

"There's no band."

"There's a jukebox. What do you want to hear?"

Grace shrugged. "Whatever you want."

He climbed off the stool and walked over to the jukebox. Two quarters and three minutes later he'd found the songs and pushed the right buttons. Then he returned to Grace and led her onto the empty dance floor. She looked as if she was humoring him. He wasn't drunk, though he wondered if he'd feel better or worse if he was. Old J.T. was alive and still causing trouble. If that wasn't a good excuse to drink himself into oblivion, he didn't know what was. But he wasn't drunk, or even tipsy. He was warm and a little on edge, but that was because he'd caught a whiff of perfume when Grace hopped off the stool and handed him the car keys.

Jack inhaled as he took Grace into his arms. He'd

punched in a slow tune, an old Willie Nelson number meant to make a man want to dance with a woman against him. She was warm and soft in his arms. His fingers spread across her back, his hand held hers. He could feel her breasts touching his chest. It sure as hell didn't feel like either one of them had much clothing on, and he'd like to take off the stuff that was in the way.

"What's wrong?"

Jack liked the way her hair tickled his chin. "What?"

"You sighed. Twice. Is something the matter?"

"No."

"This is nice," she said after Willie sang another verse.

"Yeah." He urged her another half inch closer. She felt so damn good against him. He heard himself sigh, and winced. By the time the song ended, he was a man on fire. He released her enough so he could look down into her face. "There's another song. Do you mind?"

She didn't take her hand from his shoulder. "No. Not at all."

He'd chosen another old song, this time about making love for just one night. The words took on new significance as he gathered Grace in his arms again. Several other couples joined them on the dance floor, and Jack noticed that the men gave him sympathetic smiles. He must look like a real goner, but he didn't care. He danced with Grace's tempting little body warm against his, their thighs touching, her breasts brushing his chest. He would have danced until his boots wore out, but the music eventually stopped. Some idiot had paid

for a fast tune, so Jack took Grace's hand and led her off
the dance floor as the music blasted.

"Are we leaving now?" she asked.

He paused at the edge of the crowd. "Do you want
to?"

"I should get back."

He noticed she didn't sound any more interested in
going home than he was. "Yeah," Jack said. "Thanks
for the dances."

She smiled and didn't take her hand from his. "Anytime."

He gave her the keys. "You should drive."

"Okay."

"I'm not drunk," he insisted. "But you can't be too
careful."

"Right," she said, taking the keys. He held her hand
until they reached the door and he had to drop it to
open the door to the outside. He was surprised that it
was dark. He must have been sitting in there a long
time. No wonder old Burley thought he was too plastered to drive. He'd nursed a whiskey or two, but his
presence in a bar must have reminded Burley of old
J.T.

He'd been told they looked a lot alike, and he'd
never taken that as a compliment. He climbed into the
Ford's passenger seat, rolled down his window and
watched Grace as she drove them back to the ranch. He
liked looking at her, even though he couldn't see much
in the faint glow of the dashboard lights. Her hair blew
around her face, and once in a while she glanced over
toward him.

"Did you get all of your errands done in town?"

He winced, remembering Isabella's groceries. "Not exactly. I'll have to run in tomorrow, or send one of the boys. Where is everyone, anyway?"

"Jason and Anne went to the movies, and Jet and the band headed to San Antonio to meet with a friend from Nashville. Isabella went home right after dinner, though she was grumbling about needing supplies."

He didn't want to talk about supplies. He didn't want to think about brothers, and how he might have four instead of three. When they finally reached the house, only one light in the living room glowed through the windows and the porch light illuminated the front door.

"I guess everyone is in bed," Grace said, parking the car in the shadow of the toolshed. She turned off the ignition.

Everyone was in bed but the two of them, he thought, remembering the way she'd felt against him while Willie Nelson sang. He cleared his throat and managed to say, "Thanks for the ride."

"Thanks for the dance."

It was foolish to smile at her. And it didn't make sense to reach for her in the darkness, but that's what he did. She went into his arms as if she was made for him, and he kissed her cheek and brushed her hair away from her face so he could find her lips. She tilted her head and wrapped her arms around his neck as Jack managed to avoid hurting himself on the gear shift.

It was one hell of a kiss. It continued until it was clear

to both of them that the car wasn't the best place to make love. And, Jack decided, making love was exactly what was on his mind.

SHE'D BEEN WARNED, Grace realized. She'd been told by one of the best advice-givers in Texas, and she'd done it, anyway. She'd fallen for the first real cowboy she'd met outside of Dallas. He was helping her out of her car and kissing her at the same time, which might have been because she still had her arms around his neck. He backed her against the car, his wonderful mouth on hers, his hands on her shoulders, his body warm and solid against hers.

"Crazy," he muttered, lifting his mouth.

"Us or the place?" She was afraid he was going to step away, and her heart sank as he did exactly that.

"Both," he said, taking her hand and leading her toward the house. "I don't want to make love to you against a car."

She wondered if he was teasing. "No?"

"No." She thought she heard tenderness in his voice. "I like beds or haymows, take your pick."

Grace hurried to keep up with his long strides. "Both, I suppose. I've never made love in a haymow before."

He stopped in the middle of the driveway and looked down at her with a fierce expression in his dark eyes. "Tomorrow," he promised. "You'll have your haymow tomorrow."

"And tonight?" The question was out of her mouth

before she could take it back. She'd never been bold before.

He started walking again, but he kept a gentle grip on her hand. "Tonight, Gracie, we use a bed. That is, if you're thinking what I'm thinking."

She wasn't thinking at all. That was the problem—or the wonder of it all. She decided that question didn't need an answer, especially since they were now through the front door and in an empty living room. Jack left the corner light on, tugged her down the hall and stopped in front of Grace's room. "Mac," he said.

"I'll check him," she whispered. She pushed the door open and tiptoed into the room, dark except for the wedge of light that shone from the hall. The baby was sleeping quietly, and Jimmy was sprawled on top of the bed. He was fully clothed and snoring, which presented another problem.

"Jimmy-Joe," Jack whispered, standing beside Grace. He shook his brother's shoulder until the young man opened his eyes and blinked.

"Hey," he muttered, struggling to sit up. "Must've fallen asleep."

"Thanks for watching Mac," Grace said, hoping Jimmy wouldn't notice that her cheeks were flushed and that Jack had his hand on her waist. She needn't have worried, because Jimmy muttered something about going to bed and staggered out of the room.

"Does he wake up in the night?"

She knew he was talking about the baby. "Not usually."

"My room is at the end of the hall," Jack said. "Unless you've changed your mind about the haymow."

She ignored his teasing. "I could hear Mac if he cried?"

Jack turned her toward the door. "I've heard him more than once."

"Your room, then," Grace said, knowing she'd fallen in love and it was too late to do anything to prevent it. She'd done what she'd thought she'd never do, what she was afraid would never happen to her, what she'd given up looking for. She had fallen in love for the first time in her life with a handsome rancher, a man with a gentle touch and a way of kissing that made her forget her name. She followed him down the hall and thanked her lucky stars for Texas cowboys.

The room was dark, illuminated only by an outside light that shone across the courtyard. He kicked a chair; she stumbled over the rug. Grace didn't know how they managed to get their clothes off, but it was an exciting process. He unzipped the back of her dress and eased the fabric from her shoulders. She let her dress fall to the floor while she unbuttoned Jack's shirt and kissed the base of his throat. He kissed her and caressed her, removing the remaining pieces of her clothing, until Grace stood naked near the bed. Between kisses, he somehow removed the rest of his clothes. She heard the dull thud of boots hitting the rug.

He started to lead her toward the bed, then hesitated. She wondered if he'd changed his mind. She wondered if she'd be able to face him in the morning if she had to turn around and walk, her clothes clutched to her body, back to her room. Grace braced herself for certain disappointment.

"Grace?" he whispered, fingers trailing across her rigid shoulders. "What's wrong?"

She felt foolish. She couldn't say something pathetic like *I thought you had changed your mind.* "You, um, stopped."

"I just remembered the words to Jet's song," he said, a thread of laughter running through his voice. "'Take off your boots.'"

"'Come a little bit closer'?" Grace recited, her tension easing.

"Yes, ma'am," the man said, enfolding her against his hard, warm male body. "You've got the right idea."

She should have felt self-conscious, but she didn't. Not when the backs of her knees touched the mattress, not when Jack swept the covers back and she slid between cool sheets. She didn't want to talk about boots or songs or anything else. He gathered her into his arms and ran gentle fingertips over her breasts and abdomen, then lower. Grace urged him closer. She wanted him inside her and she didn't want to wait. She'd thought she might die if she had to wait.

It was a perfect fit.

Grace didn't hide her sigh of pleasure. Jack, propped above her, brushed her lips with his. "I knew it would feel this good," he whispered.

"I didn't."

He moved within her. "No?"

She shook her head. "No."

"It gets better," he said, a smile touching his lips.

She kissed the cleft that marked his chin. "Maybe you'd better show me."

"Yes, ma'am." And he did, moving in and out in a tantalizing rhythm. Grace slid her hands to his hips as the passion built to an exquisite peak. It seemed like hours or minutes; Grace lost all sensation of time. All she knew was pleasure, loving the man whose body loved hers with such skill. She climaxed first, with Jack following with deep strokes until he shuddered into her warmth.

Long minutes later she lay snuggled against Jack's shoulder and thought about the past hour. Everything Lucy had said about cowboys was true.

10

MCLINTOCKS WEREN'T FAMILY men. Everyone knew that. There were generations of McLintocks who couldn't figure out how to stay in one place and take care of their womenfolk. They didn't fall in love and crave to be in the same bed with the same woman till the day they died.

Which was why Jack couldn't believe that he was naked and alone in his bed and very unhappy about being naked and alone in his bed. He and Grace had made love twice, and were working on the third when the baby's cries had sent Grace scrambling into her dress and out the door. Jack was left with the disappointing acceptance that further lovemaking would have to wait until later, and, for what it was worth, that he had fallen in love with his houseguest.

And he was pretty crazy about Mac, too. After all, the little guy was probably his brother. He couldn't let him go to strangers, and he couldn't let Grace find out about his father, either. No, he would have to figure out what was best for the child without revealing a truth that would hurt everyone.

It was Tuesday. Three more days and then it would be Friday morning. Jason would turn twenty-one and the lawyers would hand out checks. The party was Saturday. Grace wouldn't think about leaving until Sunday, so he had plenty of time to think over what he should do. The first thought was to keep them both here, if such a thing was possible. He and Grace could take some time and figure out just exactly what they were doing together. Yep, he might have lucked out, after all. He might have found the right woman at the right time.

Jack stretched and reached for his jeans. He might as well get some work done, now that he was awake.

"NOW, THERE'LL BE no teasing," Isabella said, shaking her spatula in Jet's direction. "It's not your business."

Jet grinned, pleased with the world today. The Nashville connection had proved to be legitimate, and the new songs were going to be recorded on demo tapes. "Can I help it if I came home in time to see Grace running out of Jack's room?"

Jason shook his head, and his fiancée smiled as if she thought the McLintocks were pretty funny. "Maybe they weren't, uh, doing it."

Jimmy nodded. "I thought I set it up pretty good, making up that story about having to stay home so she'd have to go pick him up. Do you really think old Jack spent the night with her?"

"What else would she be doing in his room at five o'clock in the morning? They hadn't been talking about the weather, I'll bet you that." Jet grinned as Isabella deposited another helping of eggs on his plate. "Thanks, Bella. I'm mighty hungry this morning."

"You're mighty mouthy, too," she said. "Talking too much about things that aren't any of your concern."

"My future sister-in-law is my concern." He winked at Anne, who gave him a shy smile. "Right, honey?"

Anne didn't answer, but Jason rolled his eyes heavenward. "You get worse every day," he said.

"Nope." Jet took a hefty swallow of coffee. "I get better. And having Jack and Grace sing together was a stroke of genius. Sending them off on a picnic was a pretty good idea, too. Our big brother needs all the help he can get in the romance department. The rest of us don't have any trouble." He shook his head. "Jack's different from the rest of us, that's for sure."

"He's had more responsibility," Isabella said. "You can't meet women when you're raising three boys."

"Well, we're raised now," Jimmy declared. "And I'm happy for him. I like Grace."

"So do I," Anne said. "But what about Mac?"

Jason met Jet's gaze. "I told her. We don't have any secrets."

His little brother had never had a secret in his life. Jet hid a sigh. "Jack could adopt him," Jet said, but even as he said it he didn't know if that was possible. There was a mystery there, a mystery that shouldn't be pried open and solved. He had the uncomfortable feeling that he didn't want to know which McLintock had been with Lucy Bagwell.

Jet picked up his coffee cup. Whatever the problem, Jack would take care of it. They all knew that.

THE MAN STEPPED OUT from behind the horse barn, causing Jack's horse to shy at the sudden movement.

Jack easily brought the horse under control, then squinted at the figure in the shadows of the building. The man lifted one hand in greeting and stepped forward out of the shadows.

"Howdy, Jack."

He didn't want to see what he was seeing. It wasn't possible. He'd been out in the sun all day long. He should have come in for lunch, but he hadn't wanted to take a chance on seeing Grace and carrying her off to bed in front of all the family. He'd ridden himself so hard he was having hallucinations.

"I hear you've been looking for me," the old bastard drawled.

Jack opened his mouth, but no sound came out. He swallowed and tried again. "What are you doing here?"

"Thought I'd wish Jason a happy birthday. Friday's his big day, isn't it?" J. T. McLintock reached into his shirt pocket and lit a hand-rolled cigarette. "Gotta quit one of these days," he muttered, giving Jack a fleeting smile.

"Smoking's the least of your problems," Jack said, dismounting. "What the hell are you doing? The last time you were on this property was after Ma died."

"She was a good woman."

"She died of overwork and a broken heart," Jack reminded the man. It was like looking into a mirror, and he hated seeing the resemblance. Thick, dark hair, wide chests and shoulders, dark eyes and heavy brows—they all matched, though his father was heavier from too many bottles of beer, and his skin was weathered and lined. He was still a handsome man; Lucy Bagwell must have thought so.

"And her father left all the money to the grandsons. My sons," the older man pointed out.

"Is that why you're here, to see if you can figure out how to get some of it?"

"Not exactly." J.T. smiled and leaned against the barn as if he had nothing better to do on a Tuesday evening. "But I hear you've been looking for me."

Jack knew better than to reply.

His father took a deep drag on the cigarette. "Yep, it seems like some lawyer's been nosing around, asking questions about me and a trip to Dallas and a redhead I once knew. Interesting questions like that." His dark-eyed gaze held Jack's. "So I got to thinking, what if this tied in with my boys' inheritance?"

Jack kept his voice and his gaze level. "I don't know what you're talking about."

"Don't you?" J.T. tossed the cigarette butt to the dirt and rubbed it out with the scuffed toe of his boot. "I thought to myself, Why would my boy be asking questions about me and that redhead? And I came up with some real interestin' answers. You want to hear them?"

"I guess you're going to tell me whether I want to hear them or not." He braced himself, but surely there was no way J.T. could know about Mac's existence.

"I saw a pretty woman holding a dark-haired baby this morning. Spittin' image of you at that age."

Leave it to J.T. to see Grace and Mac. The old man didn't miss a damn thing. "So?"

J.T. smiled and nodded, as if he'd heard what he wanted to hear. "According to Burley down at the Stampede, I don't have any grandchildren, and there's a little gal from Dallas visiting, so that brings me to what you could call a 'logical conclusion.' And I think you don't want anyone to know what that conclusion is, either."

Leave it to J.T. to get all his information while sitting on a bar stool. Jack looked over his shoulder. Last thing he needed now was any kind of an audience. The fewer people who knew J.T. was still alive, the better for everyone. "I suppose you're going to tell me."

"I ain't gonna tell anyone," he promised. "I'm going to go away nice and quiet-like."

"That always was your specialty."

"'Course, a little going-away money would help. And you and the boys are going to have plenty of it, come Friday, as long as no one knows that there's a fifth McLintock who ain't even close to being twenty-one years old."

"You're pretty sure he's a McLintock."

"Hell, son, have you taken a good look at that boy's chin? I could see it from fifty yards away."

Jack stiffened. "You can go to hell."

"I'm sure I will, someday—" the man smiled "—but I'm not goin' poor. Old Man Freemont worked me to death on this place and I never saw a dime. Seems only fair that I should get my share now. And maybe I should get my son, too. I hear Lucy died a few weeks back and that little boy is an orphan."

"What do you want?"

J.T. smiled. "So you're not denying it."

Jack cursed himself for being a fool. "I asked you what you wanted."

"Let's see, old Freemont was leaving each of his grandkids fifty thousand dollars. I'll take your share. You ended up with the ranch, anyway."

"My share of the money is going to pay off the loans." And keep the wolf from the door. And invest in some new equipment.

"Thirty thousand, then," the older man bargained. "Or I'll have a little meeting with Old Man Freemont's lawyers and see if they want to meet my fifth son."

"You're a real piece of work, J.T." He had no choice. Thirty thousand dollars was a small price to pay for his brothers' freedom. All four brothers. "Thirty thousand it is, then. But stay away from town."

"Sure. No one will ever know that there was another McLintock boy."

"And you'll stay away from here, too." He didn't want J.T. anywhere near the child or Grace or any of the boys, for that matter. "I'll get the money to you on Friday."

Jack mounted his horse. "Meet me here Friday afternoon at five."

J.T. nodded. "Nice horse."

"Yeah."

"And the ranch looks pretty good, too. You've put some money into this place."

"I've had to."

"This dump always sucked up money."

Jack looked down at his father and felt very tired. "Yeah, well, some things don't change."

MAKING LOVE WAS ONE of the world's greatest pastimes, Grace mused, watching Jack ride into the yard and dismount. Last night had been an education in just how much pleasure one woman could experience in an eight-hour period of time. They'd been quiet enough to prevent anyone from hearing them, careful enough to protect themselves against an unwanted pregnancy, and discreet enough to avoid each other today.

Everyone had been quiet today except Mac. She'd taken him for long walks outside, which seemed to please him for a while, but he was drooling and fussing again. She didn't know what she could do to make him happy. She stood by the entrance to the courtyard and held the heavy baby in her arms.

She didn't know how she was going to give him up. None of the McLintocks had come forward to claim him, which meant Mac was going to have to be given to the state authorities when she returned to Dallas. She could try adopting him herself, but an agency wasn't going to give a child to a single woman when there were so many childless couples waiting to adopt.

No, Mac needed a father. She would have to leave this wonderful home and return to Dallas. Grace didn't look forward to going back. She hadn't missed anything about her apartment. She'd called her answering machine and picked up her messages. She'd made some calls and postponed a couple of unimportant meetings. Her work could be delayed awhile longer.

No one would know she was away, except the neighbor who watered the plants and collected the mail.

Jack walked the horse toward the corral and disappeared from view.

"What's my big brother up to now?" Jet asked, coming up behind her.

"I don't know. I haven't seen him all day."

"Ranching is a full-time job."

"You're not going to miss this place when you go to Nashville?"

Jet grinned. "It's my home, but I'm ready to move on."

"All of you are ready to move on but Jack."

"He loves this place more than any of us." Jet shoved his hands in his pockets. "He's told you about the trust fund?"

"Yes. After Jason turns twenty-one. I heard about it in Locklin."

Jet chuckled. "Yeah, I guess the whole town would be talking about it. I'm glad you're staying for the party. You're good for Jack. You and Mac should stay."

Grace felt her face grow warm. She was saved from trying to come up with an answer as Jack rounded the corner of the house. His steps slowed as he noticed them waiting for him.

His gaze dropped to the sleeping baby. "Something wrong?"

"No. I think he's getting a tooth. We've been walking all afternoon."

"Give him to me." Jack moved to take Mac from her arms.

Grace hesitated. "He might wake up."

Jet stepped back so he could see Mac's face. "He's out cold. He's even drooling on your shoulder."

"He's always drooling on my shoulder." She helped Jack ease the baby out of her arms and into his. Mac blinked, made a little sound of protest, then went back to sleep. Grace rubbed her aching arms. "He's getting bigger—and heavier—every day."

Jack started toward the kitchen door. "Did I miss supper?"

"No, but Bella made five big pans of enchiladas. The Naked Ladies are joining us for dinner." Grace hurried to keep up with both men as they headed inside.

"How was San Antonio?" Jack asked, stepping into a kitchen that smelled of peppers and cheese.

"Real interesting," his brother said. "How was everything here?"

"Real quiet." Jack glanced at Grace and winked as soon as Jet turned away. "I guess I'll go clean up before supper. Want me to put Mac in his bed?"

"Sure. I'll go with you." She kept her voice casual and attempted to erase the smile from her lips. Jimmy-Joe stopped them as they left the kitchen.

"I read that screenplay," he announced. "There's a part that's perfect for me."

Grace stared up at him. If anyone was going to be an overnight sensation, it would be the handsome young cowboy standing in the kitchen doorway. "That's wonderful."

"No kidding?"

Jimmy nodded. "I talked to my agent today. He set

up a meeting for me for next Thursday. Can you believe it? My first Hollywood meeting."

"Is that like an audition?"

The young man shrugged and turned to Jack. "I guess so. They look at me and I look at them and everyone discusses the part. Boy, is this gonna be great. I can't believe it's really happening. Jimmy-Joe McLintock is going to Hollywood."

"I'd better get your autograph before you leave." Grace stood on tiptoe and kissed him on the cheek. "Congratulations. You'd better call me when you're on television so I can watch."

"I will," he promised. "I'll phone everyone I know."

"Call everyone for supper," Bella said, coming up behind him. "By the time you find everyone, it should be ready."

"Yes, ma'am."

She frowned at Jack. "You have time to clean up, if you don't dawdle."

"I'm heading that way right now," he assured her.

"I'll be right back to help," Grace said, hurrying to follow him. "I'm putting Mac to bed."

Isabella peered at the child, whose head rested heavily on Jack's shoulder. "Looks like he finally settled down," she called after them. "Maybe you'll get some sleep tonight."

Jack kept walking, but he tilted his head toward Grace. "Don't count on it," he whispered.

"DO YOU THINK they know?"

"Nope." He unbuttoned her shirt and smoothed his

hands over her lace-covered breasts. "They don't suspect a thing."

Grace loved the way he touched her. Loved the way he made her feel when he touched her. "Everyone was smiling at me tonight."

His lips found the top of one breast. "Everyone always smiles at you."

"Shh. Keep your voice down. This was different."

Her shirt fell to the floor, and her bra quickly followed. Jack turned his attention to the snap of her jeans. His fingers sent erotic sensations through her abdomen as he released the zipper and smoothed the fabric, including her underpants, past her hips. "Different?" he whispered. "How?"

"Oh, I don't know." It was getting hard to think. Especially with his lips tickling her abdomen while his fingers explored lower. It was getting pretty difficult to stand, too, when her knees threatened to dissolve from underneath her. "Take off your boots," she managed to say.

"Are you singing or giving me something to do?"

"I'm not singing. Take off your boots."

"I already did. You weren't paying attention."

Maybe not. She'd been a little mesmerized after he'd tossed his shirt over a chair and unzipped his own jeans. "Take me to bed," she whispered. "And that's not part of the song."

"Sweetheart," he said, lifting her into his arms. "I'm happy to do anything your little heart desires."

And he kept his word, too, doing things to her body that caused her to gasp with surprised pleasure.

They'd made love for the longest time, as if neither one wanted it to end. Much later, he'd come to her half asleep and she'd welcomed him into her arms and into her body. Twice in the night Grace had pulled on a nightgown and tiptoed out of the room to check on Mac. If she ran into anyone, she hoped they'd think she had been to the bathroom. But she didn't think she'd fool anyone. She looked like a woman in love, which is exactly what she was.

She'd fallen in love with a cowboy and she'd never been happier. She refused to think of the future, of what would happen after the party. The present was much too good.

"Aren't you going to open your gifts?"

Jason grinned at his fiancée. "I will, in a minute. I want to enjoy being twenty-one."

"We *all* want to enjoy that," Jet said. "This is one hell of an important day."

"We've waited a long time for you to grow up, Jase," Jimmy added.

They were seated around the dining room table, a place reserved over the years for special occasions. And this was special, all right. It wasn't every day the entire family gathered for a birthday breakfast. Jack glanced toward Grace, who sat to his right. Mac was in his high chair, between the two of them. Jack leaned over and wiped the boy's chin with his napkin.

"I have an announcement," Jason said, standing up.

Isabella, seated at the other end of the table next to

him, patted his arm. "I can't believe you are all grown up." She shook her head. "It isn't right."

"Now, Bella, I'll always be the baby of the family," he assured her. "You know that." Jason grinned as he turned to the rest of his family, including Grace in his smile, Jack noted. What on earth was the boy up to now?

"Spit it out, Jase," Jimmy said. "Before my coffee gets cold."

"Anne and I are getting married."

Jet didn't look impressed. "You told us that before, Jase."

"We're getting married tomorrow."

"Tomorrow?" Jack echoed. "*Tomorrow?*"

"Yes." Jason and Anne nodded and blushed. "We got the license last week, and we arranged for a justice of the peace to arrive tomorrow at noon."

"My parents are coming, too," Anne said. "We thought it would be easier this way."

"Married. Tomorrow." Jet grinned. "I'll have to start practicing 'Here Comes the Bride' on the guitar, now, won't I?"

Jason nodded. "That's a real good idea. I figured since we already had the party and the music and the family all in one place, we might as well make the most of it. Jack, is that okay?"

All eyes turned to the head of the table. "It's a fine idea," he said. If he could keep J.T. off the ranch, it would be one heck of an event. "If you're sure about getting married, I guess that's what you'd better do."

Relief swept across Jason's face, and he sat down

and put his arm around Anne. "Thanks, everyone," he said, his grin widening. "I told Anne you guys wouldn't mind."

Grace looked down the table at Anne. "What about a dress?"

"I saw one in town yesterday, but I didn't have time to try it on. I thought I'd go in this morning and shop."

"Do you want company?"

Anne smiled her familiar shy smile. "I'd like that."

Isabella nodded. "I'll keep Mac with me so you girls can shop. Buy Jason a new shirt, too, will you?"

"We will," Grace promised, looking happy.

Jack shook his head. Leave it to women to be happy about shopping.

"What about you, Jack? Do you want to celebrate your good fortune and a wedding by getting a new shirt?"

"No. I have plenty of shirts."

Grace shot him a questioning look, which he tried to ignore by picking up his coffee cup.

"I thought you'd be happy today. What's going on?" she asked him.

"Nothing." He'd spent yesterday afternoon in his office, trying to figure out how to make twenty thousand dollars pay off thirty-five thousand in bank loans. The drop in cattle prices, the 1993 tornados and Jason's education had taken their toll. He'd kept the place afloat for twenty years. He would have to sell the east section to his neighbor now.

"I don't believe you."

"Drop it, Grace. Nothing is wrong."

"It's Mac, isn't it." She kept her voice low while the others teased Jason about becoming an old married man. "You know something."

"No." But he heard the lie in his own voice and he couldn't meet her eyes.

"Jack? Who does Mac belong to?"

The voices silenced as the others heard her question and looked to him for an answer. Jack looked at his brothers, at the sympathetic expression on Bella's lined face, at the surprise that flitted across Anne's. He couldn't look at Grace, but he turned to Mac. He'd planned to protect him. He may as well start now.

Jack took a deep breath and met Grace's eyes. "He's mine."

"Yours."

"Mine," he repeated, a little louder this time. "Mac is mine. He's a genuine McLintock."

The genuine McLintock started to cry, so Grace lifted him from the high chair and into her arms. "He can't be. You said—"

"I was wrong."

No one else at the table dared contradict him.

Grace stood up and put Mac in Jack's lap. "Then you might as well start taking care of him." She sat down and picked up her coffee cup as if nothing had happened. Mac reached for Jack's napkin and tried to put it in his mouth.

"Hey," Jack said. "Stop that." Mac looked up at him and smiled.

"I'll bet you found your dress in the Crystal Butterfly," Grace said to Anne.

"Uh, yes, I think that was the name."

Jack stood up, Mac secure in his arms. "We have a meeting at the bank in two hours, boys. I suggest we be on time."

The brothers nodded and almost knocked each other down trying to leave the table.

"YOU'RE LYING," GRACE said, poking her finger at Jack's chest. "And don't think I don't know it."

He backed up a step. "Why would I lie about this?"

"I don't know." And she really didn't, though she had a few ideas. "You're protecting one of the boys, and that's not right. One of them should be made to accept responsibility for his actions."

"Jet had the mumps and can't have kids," Jack reminded her. "And Jimmy-Joe was in a play *and* had a jealous girlfriend at the time of Mac's conception."

"Which leaves you and Jason."

"Jason doesn't count," Jack said a little too quickly.

"You're taking Mac so Jason can get married and live happily ever after? Isn't that a little extreme? Anne would make a great mother, and Jason would be a wonderful father. He reads stories to Mac all the time. They're a little young, but—"

"Mac is a McLintock and he's mine. And Jason might not be the only McLintock who wants to settle down."

"Meaning?" He couldn't be saying what she thought he was.

"Meaning," he said, giving her a brief kiss, "I need

to get these next two days over with before I can start thinking about myself. And us. And Mac."

"Us?" She loved the word *us*.

He put his large hands on her shoulders and made her look at him. "Let me get the boys on their way. Then you and I will sit in the courtyard and talk about the future, okay, Grace?"

She could do nothing else but nod her head yes. "And then, the truth."

"When the dust settles, Gracie. Then I'll tell you everything."

Grace watched him walk out of the bedroom. She planned to hold him to that promise.

11

"WHY ARE YOU DOING this, Jack?" Jet stood beside his older brother in the lobby of Locklin Federal Savings Bank.

"Doing what?"

"Is Mac really Jason's, after all?"

"No."

"And he's not yours," Jet said. "I'd bet my own mother that you didn't leave Lucy What's-her-name pregnant and alone."

Jack smiled wryly. "Why not? It seems to run in the family."

"Not this generation."

The brothers stood in silence and watched the younger boys at the bank tellers' windows. Jet patted his shirt pocket. "I have a check in here that will finance a year or two in Nashville, more if I'm careful. Jason has his studies in Europe. Jimmy should be able to make it in L.A. What are you doing with your money, Jack? Putting it back in the ranch?"

"Yeah, you could say that." Along with a fat donation to Father of the Year.

"You could take Grace somewhere nice. You could go to New Orleans. I'll bet she'd like all those old buildings with the balconies. Or what about heading up to the mountains, to Utah?"

"You have some pretty strange ideas, Jet."

"You're not in love with her, then?"

Jack looked at his watch. He could still get in a few hours' work if they could get home. "I didn't say that."

"You have an odd way of showing it, brother. Are you taking Mac to make Grace happy?"

"Not exactly, but that's part of it, I guess." Jack took a deep breath. "I'm going to ask Grace to marry me, soon as the party is over and the place gets back to normal. She takes good care of that baby, but I don't know if she wants to be his mother permanently. And I'm not real sure how she feels about me."

"Have you told her you loved her?"

"Well, no."

Jet shrugged. "Guess I can't blame you there. That's getting in pretty deep."

"I'm going to do my best to convince her to take on an old cowboy and a less-than-profitable ranch, but she has a business in Dallas. She has a whole life I don't even know about."

Jet clapped him on the back. "Looks like you've got plenty of time to find out, once you've walked down the aisle."

"Shut up," Jack said, but there was affection in the command. He looked around to see if anyone had overheard Jet's comment about walking down the aisle. "There's just one McLintock getting married right now, and he's coming toward us with a grin plastered all over his face."

"I can afford to buy a ring now," Jason proudly announced.

Jack tried to keep a straight face. "That sounds like a good idea."

"Can you afford to buy your brothers a beer, too?"

"Yeah," Jimmy said, joining them in time to hear the last suggestion. "We need a bachelor party."

"Just one beer," Jack cautioned. "I have cattle to feed."

"Sure, Jack." Jet winked at the other three. "We'll feed those cattle as soon as we're through in town."

Jack nodded toward Harry White, the banker, who gave him the thumbs-up sign from his corner office door, and followed his brothers out of the bank. On Monday he'd take care of business; a check for thirty thousand was folded in his shirt pocket. A small price to pay for Grace and Mac's happiness, the check would be delivered at five o'clock to J.T.

And then Jack would start the rest of his life.

"I NOW PRONOUNCE YOU husband and wife."

Grace blinked back tears as the justice of the peace—who looked more like Johnny Cash than Johnny Cash—finished conducting the courtyard wedding ceremony. Anne looked lovely in a simple white sundress and a white cowgirl hat decorated with satin ribbon and pink rosebuds. Jason wore a new pair of blue jeans, a white western shirt and a black string tie. Both the bride and groom, now kissing each other with shy pleasure, wore cowboy boots.

The audience applauded, with several members of

the Naked Ladies hooting their approval. Jet strummed a few chords on his electric guitar and began an instrumental version of "Look At Us," Vince Gill's anniversary ballad. Fitting, Grace decided, reaching for a tissue while balancing Mac on her hip. The baby was fascinated by all of the people. He didn't seem to mind being passed around to Isabella's daughters and granddaughters, all of whom claimed the right to care for him. Isabella, resplendent in a bright pink dress, openly wept into a large handkerchief while Jimmy-Joe tried to comfort her.

Jack, the best man, stood near the Johnny Cash lookalike and watched Jason and his bride wade through the crowd. Everyone wanted to congratulate Jason and kiss Anne. Anne's parents, a sweet couple from Austin, seemed to be enjoying the boisterous celebration. Grace's gaze returned to Jack, who looked too serious. Worried, even, as he scanned the crowd as if searching for someone in particular. She didn't understand what was going on, but she looked forward to hearing his explanation.

He'd stayed away from her bed. And she'd stayed away from his. There was an unspoken agreement that everything—even sex—was on hold until the weekend was over. She missed him. And she would miss the baby in her arms, too. Going back to Dallas was starting to feel like punishment. She didn't dare let herself think that she would stay with Jack, here in Locklin, with Mac and maybe several McLintock children with dark hair and charming smiles.

She'd never thought she'd be one of the lucky ones,

those women with adoring husbands and happy children and a house that rang with excited chatter. She'd only dreamed of a large family, with uncles and aunts and cousins arriving on holidays.

Well, dreams were dreams, and reality was that little apartment in Dallas.

But love was here on the ranch, here with Jack McLintock. She blinked as he stepped closer and stood by her side.

"Is everything all right?" he asked.

"Just fine."

"Are you having a good time?"

He was treating her like a casual guest, instead of someone who'd strung lights across the eaves and rearranged the pots of flowers this morning. "It's a lovely party."

"It's just getting started." He pointed to Jet and the band. "They're going to set up out back and turn up the volume now, so hang on." Jack peered at the baby. "Hey, kid. How do you like your first party?"

"He likes it, especially when Lina's daughters take him for walks."

"Want me to take him?"

"Not yet. He needs his diaper changed, so I'm going to go clean him up and try putting him to bed at Lina's for a while. The girls said they'd stay with him, and it's a little quieter over there."

"Good. You'll come back and dance with me?"

Grace smiled. He sounded like an unsure teenager. "After I help Bella put the food out, sure. How about one of Jet's belly-rubbing songs?"

"Jet's *what?*"

"A slow dance," she explained, happy to have flustered him. She moved toward the house. "I'll see you in a little while."

He nodded and looked relieved. "Hurry back. There are some folks I'd like you to meet."

"Okay." She would meet the devil himself if Jack would keep looking at her with that tender expression on his face.

"THAT'S A PRETTY good-looking woman you've got yourself. And that's another fine-looking boy I sired," she heard a man drawl from outside the door to the courtyard. Grace leaned over the bed and slipped the plastic pants over Mac's chubby thighs. So far he showed no sign of being sleepy, which didn't bode well for his afternoon nap.

"Stay away from both of them," Jack said, sounding angry. At least, Grace thought the voice belonged to Jack. She'd never heard him sound that upset before, except maybe when the man at the Stampede had threatened him. What on earth was the visitor talking about? Obviously this wasn't one of the people Jack wanted to introduce her to.

"Why didn't you show up yesterday? I waited at the barn for over an hour before I started thinking you finally grew a conscience and changed your mind."

"I got a little sidetracked in San Antonio."

"You have no business being here today when half the town is wandering around. What if someone recognizes you?"

Grace sat down on the bed and listened carefully. She didn't know what was going on.

"You kidding? Everybody's gathering around the food and the beer, or they're off dancing to Jet's crazy music. I'll keep my hat low and my sunglasses on, son, if that makes you happy."

Son? Grace tried to remember what Jack had said about his father. She'd assumed he was dead, but had Jack said that exactly?

"Thanks," the man said. "You boys enjoy the rest of Freemont's check, you hear?"

"Get out," Jack said, his voice low. Grace strained to hear his next words. "You sure as hell don't belong here."

"I loved your mother," the man said, sounding a little sad. "But I wasn't the right man for her."

"Get out," Jack repeated, sounding as if he was talking through gritted teeth. "*Now*, before I change my mind."

There was a chuckle. "You won't change your mind. You've got what you want, too, and so do your brothers. As long as I don't tell anyone that kid is mine, you and the boys are rich. Looks like we're both going to have a good weekend. I'll think I'll get a beer. For the road."

"Out," Jack repeated. "And don't talk to any of the others."

"See you around, kid."

Grace hurried to put Mac in his bed so she could go to the window and see the man Jack had been talking to. She didn't dare think what the words had meant.

She couldn't let herself think that she'd heard that Mac was that man's child. *Another fine-looking boy I sired* were his words. *You and the boys are rich.*

She opened the door to the courtyard before she thought better of it. Jack turned, his mouth in a grim line.

"Oh, hell."

"So there's another McLintock, after all," Grace said, her voice sounding calm. He couldn't know her heart was threatening to pound so hard she couldn't hear her own words. "I guess I should have figured it out for myself."

"I thought you went to Lina's," he said, sounding resigned.

"No." She waited there in the shade of the overhang, in between two pots of yellow chrysanthemums, for some kind of explanation, but Jack simply stared at the crowd of people by the kitchen end of the courtyard. "That man is your father?"

He hesitated, then replied. "Yes."

"I thought all along you were protecting Jason."

Mac started to cry, so Grace turned toward her bedroom. She looked back over her shoulder at the tall rancher. "You've been lying all along."

"Yes, but I had my reasons." He didn't bother to deny it. "We need to talk."

"No," she said, going inside to the crying child. "We don't have anything else to say." She shut the door, muffling the outside noise and effectively shutting Jack outside. He could have opened the door and followed her, but she didn't think he'd really want to start confessing how he'd known all along who Mac's father was. It didn't take a genius to figure out that none of the McLintocks wanted to wait another twenty-one years for their inheritance, and if Jack's father announced he had another son, then that's exactly what could happen. The party would be over. And so would Nashville, Hollywood and Oxford.

One little baby would have changed everything.

One little baby *had* changed everything, especially for her.

Well, she'd had it with the McLintocks and their lies. They'd fooled her, with their poems and songs and stories and picnics. Jack must have laughed as she believed everything he told her.

Grace soothed the wailing baby and tossed clothes from the dresser onto the bed. Her bags were under the bed; she quickly filled them with clothes and managed to zip them shut. She and Mac were going to get out of here. She'd thought the boy should be with his father, but that had been another silly fantasy.

There was no such thing as the perfect family.

"HAS ANYONE SEEN GRACE?"

Jimmy-Joe shook his head. "I thought she was in the kitchen."

"No, I looked. Isabella hasn't seen her, and neither has Jason." He'd looked everywhere. She wasn't in her bedroom or at Lina's house.

"And Mac? Wherever that baby is, that's where Grace will be." Jimmy poured himself another beer from the keg packed in ice. "Hey, don't worry. She'll turn up. This is a great party."

"We had an argument," Jack said, his eyes scanning the crowd.

"Yeah?" He took a sip of the beer and frowned. "Nothing serious, I hope."

"No," Jack lied, not meeting his brother's eyes. "Nothing serious." He roamed through the crowd, shook hands with some old friends, pretended he was having a good time. He kept looking for Grace, or for someone who might have seen her, and ended up at the foot of the bandstand. He drew his finger across his neck so Jet would know to end the song, and Jet nodded.

After he announced they were taking a break, he hopped off the stage. "Hey, Jack, what's wrong?"

Jack tried to sound casual. "I can't find Grace or Mac anywhere. Thought you might have a better vantage point from the stage."

Jet tilted his hat off his face. "Shoot, Jack, you look like hell. They're probably over at Lina's trying to get the baby to sleep."

"I checked. I've checked everywhere."

His younger brother's eyes narrowed. "You two have a fight?"

"Yeah."

"Why?"

Jack hesitated. He didn't want to spoil a good party, but his heart was in his throat and he felt like he could punch something. If he didn't find Grace soon, then he was going to go out of his mind with worry. "J.T. was here."

Jet's mouth dropped open. "I thought the old man was dead."

"He's very much alive. Unfortunately."

"What's this got to do with Grace?" He lifted the guitar strap over his head and set the instrument in its case.

"She overheard some things she shouldn't have."

"What the hell are you talking about?" And then, before Jack could answer, realization lit Jet's eyes. "Mac."

"Yeah."

Jet continued to look shocked. "J.T. doesn't *want* him, does he?"

"Hell, no. He blackmailed me into giving him some money in exchange for leaving Mac alone."

"You gave him money? How much money?"

"Look, I'll explain later. After I talk to Grace."

Jet whistled. "You should have told us. We could have helped you out. We all will—"

"I can't talk about this now, Jet."

"Have you looked for her car?"

"There's no way she could get out of here. There's no way any of us can. Have you seen how many cars are parked in front of the shed?" Even as he said the words, he knew that if Grace wanted to leave she would have figured out how to do it. Jack looked at the barn.

"You can't ride a horse to Dallas," Jet pointed out, reading his mind.

"No," Jack said, looking toward the outhouse. "But I can take a bus."

"No, Jack. It won't—"

"Yes, it will." If that woman thought she could leave him without a word, she had another think coming. He'd waited to say what he wanted to say long enough. When a McLintock made up his mind, the world better watch out. Besides, he was tired of waiting for his life to begin.

"DON'T FALL IN LOVE with a cowgirl," she told the sleepy baby. "She'll break your heart, just like the cowboys do."

Mac blinked and yawned.

"Your mama was a wise woman, except she should have picked someone else to make sure you had a daddy." Grace gripped the steering wheel and eased her foot off the gas. Anger was making her drive three miles an hour over the speed limit. "I sure haven't done a very good job of it."

She'd had her heart broken by a cowboy, just as Lucy had warned. She'd climbed into bed with the handsomest cowhand in Texas and what had happened?

"Disaster," she answered out loud. "Nothing but disaster from start to finish."

Mac closed his eyes, seemingly comforted by the motion of the car and the sound of her voice.

"What am I going to do with you now?" She would get a fancy lawyer and she would petition the court for custody. She would do everything in her power to adopt Mac. She'd tried giving him to his family, but they'd pretended he wasn't theirs. Their lives would be simpler if he didn't exist.

And he wouldn't exist. He would become Mac Daniels and live with his new mommy in Dallas. Maybe she would buy a house with a nice yard, and trees for a swing and a tree house. No, maybe not a tree house. She didn't know how kids kept from falling out of those things.

She heard honking behind her, but she paid no attention. The road was clear. Anyone could pass.

Anyway, it would be the two of them, forever. Or at least until Mac got married. She would see that he grew up to be the kind of man who would never, ever lie to a woman. She would make sure he married someone very nice and deserving of him.

Honk, honk. Grace looked in the rearview mirror. A blue bus was driving too close to her and honking like there was no tomorrow. "Go around, dummy," she muttered, returning her gaze to the stretch of highway ahead of her. "You're going to wake my baby."

Honk, honk, honk.

She looked in the rearview mirror again. It was a blue bus with the hand of a woman painted over the driver's side of the window. Her rings were blue and green, and Grace knew that on the side of the bus that painted woman would be naked, except for a strategically placed set of drums.

"Oh, no." She shook her head, hoping whoever was driving would get the message. She flipped her mirror up and gripped the steering wheel. He couldn't make her pull over.

Of course he could, she realized in less than ten minutes. He could stay behind her and honk that horn until she wanted to pull over into a rest area and get out of the car just so she could scream at him to stop. Which is what she did.

"Just what do you think you're doing, terrorizing someone on the highway?" She put her hands on her hips and glared as Jack hopped out of the bus. "And why are you driving that crazy bus? Does Jet know you stole it?"

"It was about time you stopped," Jack said, approaching her. His boots made crunching noises in the gravel. "I didn't know how much gas was left in this thing. Just where the hell did you think you were going?"

"Back home. Where I belong."

He got within two feet of her and stopped, crossing his arms across his chest. "And taking my son with you? No way."

"He's not your son."

"Who says? I believe the birth certificate says 'J. McLintock.'"

"You and I both know you're not that McLintock. You've been lying since the first time I met you."

"Not exactly. I thought one of the boys was Mac's father, but after that didn't work out, I had some investigating done."

"And you found out who Mac's father really was."

He nodded. "That's right."

"You're *proud* of it?" She couldn't believe him. Jack

stood there calmly, as if they were discussing the price of beef.

"Well, I'm not proud of having J.T. for a father, that's for sure. But do you think I would let him have Mac? No way."

"He wanted Mac? What are you talking about?"

He took a step toward her and Grace backed up. A woman walking her tiny dog eyed them curiously.

"You okay over there?" she called.

"I'm fine, thank you," Grace said, trying to smile.

"Will you stop acting like I'm some kind of violent criminal?" He shoved his hands in his pockets. "Look, Gracie, all I want is for you and that boy to be happy."

Grace felt like she was missing something. "You didn't lie so you could get the money?"

Jack winced. "There isn't a lot of money left, honey. I gave most of it to J.T. to keep him out of our lives, and I'll pay off some of the loans with the rest. I still have to sell part of—"

Relief flooded through her. "You gave him your money to keep Mac?"

"Not 'gave,' exactly. It was more like blackmail, but yes, J.T. is richer tonight. I'm back to square one again, but it looks like beef prices are going up. We'll make out all right." He smiled that charming McLintock smile. "I don't mind if you don't."

"Why should I mind?" she whispered.

His smile disappeared. He lifted her chin with one finger and looked into her eyes. "Being married to a cowboy might not be the life you want."

"Is that a proposal?"

"It sure as hell is, sweetheart. And I've never asked a woman to marry me before, so be gentle."

"I've never been asked before, so be nice. I'm thinking."

Jack frowned. "Either you say yes or you don't."

"Not about that. About money. I can sell my apartment," she said. "That ought to buy a few more cows."

He raised his eyebrows. "You want to be a rancher?"

"You're marrying a woman with assets. I'll want to invest in our business." She decided against telling him about the savings accounts and the mutual funds. She'd save some surprises for later. "Okay?"

Jack nodded, his dark eyes twinkling. "All right, but you have to learn how to ride a horse."

"Agreed." Grace touched his face with her fingertips. "Do you think all of our babies will have your chin?"

"Only if you come home with me right now." He smiled and swept her into his arms.

Some day, Gracie, you'll meet a man who will make your little heart pound faster than a runaway train. And when that happens, honey, hang on and enjoy the ride.

_____ Epilogue _____

"BLOW OUT THE CANDLES and make a wish," Grace urged him. "Go ahead, it's okay."

Mac leaned forward and puffed his cheeks. He released the air, and the four candles flickered and went out. Everyone clapped, and Jack, poised across the table, clicked the camera shutter. Mac scrambled down from the chair and hurried over to his father. "Show me," he said, and then, remembering his manners, added, "Please."

"This isn't that kind of camera, Mac. Sorry."

Mac sighed. "Okay," he said, and ran back to his seat. "I want cake, too," he reminded his mother. "Please."

Grace cut thick wedges of cake for everyone and passed them around the table. They were all here for the party, though it was calving season, too. The boys came home each March, not so much because Jack needed the help, but because they all liked to work together once a year.

"Tell us about New York," Bella said, turning to Jason. "Are they treating you well at that fancy school?"

"Yes, Bella. You'll come to see me get my degree, won't you? Anne's hoping everyone will come."

Jimmy stuck him with a fork. "Don't expect us to start calling you *Dr.* McLintock."

Jet stole Jimmy's cake while he wasn't looking. "Hey, we'll all be there. I've got a tour starting next month, but I made sure we'd be on the East Coast the first weekend of May."

"I love the new song, Jet. I hear it on the radio all the time." Grace cut another piece of cake and slid it in front of Jimmy. He looked too thin, but he was tanned and as handsome as ever. "What about you? Can you get away from those fancy starlets long enough to fly to New York?"

"Yeah, no problem. Anyone catch the show last week? I got to kiss Heather Locklear."

Jack chuckled. "We saw. You looked like you were enjoying yourself."

"She looks like a real babe," Jet agreed. "But can she sing?"

Everyone laughed while Jimmy shook his head. "I can't help it if I date actresses. Everybody in L.A. is an actor."

"I saw your picture in one of the supermarket tabloids again. You took somebody famous to the Academy Awards." Grace struggled to sit down in her chair. The next McLintock was due to make an appearance in two weeks, which couldn't happen soon enough as far as she was concerned. Her back ached miserably, and she'd gotten so she was jealous of every cow that dropped her calf. She smiled at the worried expression on her husband's face. "I'm fine. Stop looking like that."

"Nah, they had it wrong," Jimmy-Joe was saying. "I took a very nice lady to a very nice party to *watch* the Oscars."

"I'm sure you did," Bella said, patting his hand. Lina and her daughters laughed at the face he made at them.

"Mommy! Presents!" Mac patted a pile of brightly wrapped gifts. "They mine?"

"Go ahead," Grace said, trying to get comfortable on the chair so she could see every smile that crossed her son's face. He ripped apart paper and boxes to reveal Matchbox cars, a toddler-proof tape player with a thick plastic microphone, a set of storybooks with extra-strong pages and a bright bucket of oversized connecting blocks.

Mac clapped his hands and screamed with joy as each gift emerged from its wrapping. "T'ank you, t'ank you," he cried, with kisses for everyone.

"One more," Grace told him. "Jet, behind you is a big blue box. Can you reach it for me?" He leaned over and placed the box in front of Mac. "Go on, open it," Grace said. "It's from someone very special."

Jack shot her a questioning look and leaned closer. "What's going on?"

"I found it with Lucy's things when we emptied her apartment. I know she meant it for Mac."

"Very nice," Jack said, nodding his approval. "You think up the damnedest things."

"Ooh, a horse like Daddy's!" Mac held up a stuffed brown horse whose mane and tail were made of thick black yarn. He sported a black vinyl saddle, miniature stirrups and plastic reins. "I a cowboy," the child announced.

His uncle Jet winked at him. "The ladies love cowboys, Mac, my boy."

"Don't tell him that," Grace laughed, and then felt a strange sensation wash over her. "Oh, no."

Jack was on his feet in an instant. "What's wrong?"

"I think my water broke."

His arm was around her, his face close to hers. "Oh, hell, Gracie. Now what do we do?"

She couldn't help smiling as a feeling of calm swept over her. Everything would always turn out fine as long as Jack was with her. She turned to the sea of worried faces, her family, and announced, "I guess we're about to have another McLintock."

Isabella clapped her hands with glee. Jason smiled. Jimmy-Joe turned white, and Jet shook his head. "Leave it to a rancher to have a baby during calving season."

Hearts mend, Gracie. And life goes on, just the way it was meant to.

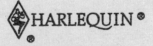

Take 4 bestselling love stories FREE

Plus get a FREE surprise gift!

As Seen on TV!

Free Gift Offer

With a Free Gift proof-of-purchase
from any Harlequin® book, you can receive
a beautiful cubic zirconia pendant.

This stunning marquise-shaped stone is a genuine cubic
zirconia—accented by an 18" gold tone necklace.
(Approximate retail value $19.95)

Send for yours today...
compliments of ◈HARLEQUIN®

Free Gift Certificate

Name: _____

Address: _____

City: _____ State/Province: _____ Zip/Postal Code: _____

FREE GIFT OFFER   084-KEZ

ONE PROOF-OF-PURCHASE
To collect your fabulous FREE GIFT, a cubic zirconia pendant, you must include this original proof-of-purchase for each gift with the properly completed Free Gift Certificate.

084-KEZ

Temptation®

COMING NEXT MONTH

#629 OUTRAGEOUS Lori Foster
Blaze

One minute, a sexy-as-sin cop is rescuing Emily Cooper from drunken hoodlums. Five minutes later, he's tearing his clothes off in front of a group of voracious women. What kind of man is he... and why can't Emily keep her hands off him? Little does she know that Judd Sanders really *is* a cop, whose "cover" leaves him a little too *uncovered* for his liking!

#630 ONE ENCHANTED NIGHT Debra Carroll
It Happened One Night...

Lucy Weston doesn't believe her aunt can conjure up a man from her dusty book of love spells, but she agrees to help try. Soon after, there's a knock at the door, and a gorgeous, unconscious man falls into her arms. Before long the sexy stranger has also fallen into Lucy's bed. But no one, not even her fantasy lover, knows who he is....

#631 TWICE THE SPICE Patricia Ryan
Double Dare

Meet shy, studious Emma Sutcliffe and her flamboyant identical twin, Zara. And see what happens when Emma reluctantly takes on her sister's identity, her daring clothes and a risky adventure with the sexiest man she's ever met. And then, next month, don't miss Harlequin Intrigue #420, *Twice Burned*, for Zara's gripping story.

#632 THE TROUBLE WITH TONYA Lorna Michaels

Tonya Brewster is a walking disaster area. She can't hold a job, isn't capable of driving within the speed limit and hasn't had a date in who knows how long! But when she sets her sights on rugged, hunky Kirk Butler, he doesn't stand a chance. Because Kirk has no idea just how *much* trouble Tonya can be....

AVAILABLE NOW:

#625 THE NEXT MAN IN TEXAS
Kristine Rolofson

#626 AFTER THE LOVING
Sandy Steen

#627 THE HONEYMOON DEAL
Kate Hoffmann

#628 POSSESSING ELISSA
Donna Sterling

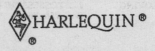